The Ice Company

The Ice Company

by
G.-J. Arnaud

adapted into English by
Jean-Marc & Randy Lofficier

A Black Coat Press Book

ISBN 978-1-935558-31-6. First Printing. February 2010. Published by Black Coat Press, an imprint of Hollywood Com-
ics.com, LLC, P.O. Box 17270, Encino, CA 91416. All rights
reserved. Except for review purposes, no part of this book may
be reproduced or transmitted in any form or by any means,
electronic or mechanical, including photocopying, recording,
or by any information storage and retrieval system, without
permission in writing from the publisher. The stories and characters depicted in this novel are entirely fictional. Printed in
the United States of America.

Foreword

Georges-Camille Arnaud, better known as G.-J. Arnaud, was born on July 3, 1928, in St. Gilles-du-Gard, in the picturesque region of the Camargue in Southern France. He is sometimes confused with Georges Arnaud, the nom-de-plume of Henri Girard, who wrote the well-known thriller *Le Salaire de la Peur* [*The Wages of Fear*].

Arnaud is one of France's most prolific writers, the author of well over 350 popular literature novels in different genres, including espionage thrillers, detective fiction, science fiction, horror, erotic fiction, and mainstream literature.

His first novel was a detective novel entitled *Ne tirez pas sur l'Inspecteur* [*Don't Shoot at the Detective*], published in 1952 under the nom-de-plume of "Saint-Gilles." It won Arnaud the coveted Award of the Quai des Orfèvres, named after the Parisian address of the Police Judiciaire, and he continued to write detective novels under that name, as well as that of "Georges Murey."

The 1950s being the era of the Cold War, espionage novels were also very popular, and Arnaud, this time using the pseudonym of "Gil Darcy," embarked on a series of spy novels featuring the character of Luc Ferran for publisher L'Arabesque.

In 1960, Arnaud joined the writing stable of Editions Fleuve Noir, one of France's leading paperback publisher, which had been founded in 1949 by Armand de Caro and Guy Krill, and published several monthly imprints devoted to police thrillers, espionage novels, adventure novels, science fiction and horror novels.

Fleuve Noir's policy was to rely on a team of steady house authors, whose pseudonyms were owned by the publisher.

Arnaud quickly became one of Fleuve Noir's more prolific authors, starting with *Virus* (*Spécial-Police* No. 260, 1960) and *Forces Contaminées* [*Contaminated Forces*] (*Espionnage* No. 274, 1961). He won the Golden Palm for Espionage Novels in 1966 for *Les Égarés* [*The Lost Ones*] (*Espionnage* No. 573) and the 1977 Critics' Mystery Award for *Enfantasme* (*Spécial-Police* No. 1235, 1960), which was later adapted into a motion picture by Sergio Gobbi under the title *L'Enfant de Nuit* [*The Night Child*].

Arnaud's signature character for the *Espionnage* imprint, Commander Serge Kovacs, a rather anarchistic French secret service agent specializing in sensitive operations, became so popular that several novels were adapted in the graphic novel format in the 1970s.

Arnaud made his first appearance in the *Anticipation* imprint in 1971 with *Les Croisés de Mara* [*The Crusaders of Mara*], the first volume of a trilogy comprised of Nos. 469, 509 and 538, entitled *Chroniques de la Longue Séparation* [*Chronicles of the Long Separation*], in which a group of characters from the lost human colony of Mara, which has reverted to feudalism, rediscover their origins and then embark on a quest through space to find Earth.

The *Ice Company* series, the sprawling saga of a future Earth that lives under a new Ice Age, ruled by powerful, oligarchic rail companies, began in 1980 with *La Compagnie des Glaces* (*Anticipation* No. 997) and continued until 2006, winning Arnaud the 1982 French Science Fiction Grand Prize and the 1988 Apollo Award.

ANTICIPATION

FICTION

G.J. ARNAUD

LES CROISES DE MARA

FLEUVE NOIR

For its sheer scope, complexity, ambition, and unrivalled craftsmanship, *The Ice Company* ranks with such established masterpieces as Isaac Asimov's *Foundation* and Frank Herbert's *Dune* series. It became an unprecedented publishing phenomenon in French science fiction, inspiring a popular role-playing game, a graphic novel series, and finally, in 2007, a French-Canadian co-produced animated television series, sold overseas under the name *Grand Star*, which reinterpreted most of Arnaud's universe in order to target young viewers.

In 1987, at the behest of one of Fleuve Noir's managing directors, the undersigned tried to sell an English-language edition of *The Ice Company*, translating the first book in the series, and presenting an overview of the next 33 volumes. Sadly, the daunting amount of material available scared all the American publishers who reviewed the package, unwilling to commit to such a long-running series. We would like to think that the ever-growing success of *The Ice Company* in the 1990s and 2000s shows that our instinct was right.

It is that translation, and a slightly updated version of the overview, which are included in this volume.

Jean-Marc & Randy Lofficier

THE ICE COMPANY

CHAPTER ONE

Lien Rag had been waiting for over an hour to see the Military Security Lieutenant. From the anteroom, he could see all of Grand Star Station. The view was so encompassing that it rivaled any which could be had from the dispatching towers. The rails disappeared into the distance, farther than the eye could see, until they reached the fake horizon, which was nothing more than the curvature of the city dome, miles away.

Distractedly, Lien looked up and saw the Ice People, three hundred feet above him. They lived outside the dome and spent their lives cleaning it in exchange for food and trinkets. They were naked, or almost naked, and could withstand the incredible sub-zero temperatures of the outside world. Lien saw four of them, all men. In spite of their thick, reddish fur and their loincloths, their genitals, long and dangling between their legs, were clearly visible. One day, by accident, the wife of a governor or director of the Company had looked up at the dome and, discovering their nudity, taken offense. Security had tried to get the Redfurs, as they were commonly called, to wear clothes, but the Ice People could not get used to something that was, to them, totally alien and restrictive. So, a compromise had been suggested; they were to wear loincloths while working on the dome.

A fat man with a ruddy complexion was waiting with Lien in the anteroom. He, too, looked up, then shrugged.

"What a life, naked at fifty below, clearing off snow. If we just heated the dome, we wouldn't need them anymore."

"But it would be more expensive for the Company," Lien explained.

"Are you here to get a red box, Voyager?"

"No," Lien replied, annoyed by the other man's indiscretion.

"Mine blew up the other day, and now they're accusing me of sabotage... I'm a meat wholesaler and I'm on the rails all the time, but my wife lives in Lake Station..."

It was a small town up north, near a naturally-warm water lake created by a spring deep beneath the ice. Rumor had it that a buried nuclear reactor was the cause of this phenomenon, but since there were no signs of radioactivity, Lien didn't really believe it.

"It's nice there. Life is pretty comfortable... But I'm only there a day or two a week. Still... My wife comes and joins me sometimes. She's got a loco-car. I wouldn't mind spending more time there."

He must make a lot of money, thought Lien, who never had a penny to his name.

"Excuse me," he said.

His name had just appeared in bright letters on the black door of the Lieutenant's office. The latter was a small oriental, plump and hunched over. He was wearing old-fashioned glasses, but Lien thought it was probably an affectation. It was hardly likely that Security would promote someone who was near-sighted.

"You're Lien Rag, a Class-2 Glaciologist? I see here that you've applied for a steam engine. But I need some more information before I can process your file."

"Of course," Lien said, carefully. "You see, Lieutenant Skoll..."

He had just read the Security man's name on his red accented, black jacket.

"... My work sometimes forces me to travel on old, abandoned lines that are no longer electrified..."

"You have batteries."

"Yes, but they only give me a limited amount of freedom, whereas with a steam engine, I could travel to deserted areas where the ice is still pure."

Lieutenant Skoll took off his glasses and wiped them with his handkerchief. Lien Rag thought that, at one time or another, he must have seen an old motion picture, and obviously enjoyed copying the gestures of some long-dead actor.

"What lines are you planning to travel on then, Glaciologist?"

"They're all listed in my application, Lieutenant. As you can see, I'm only using official documents from the Company's archives."

"Of course, of course. You've never heard of a line called the 'Oblique Road,' I suppose?"

Lien answered without hesitating.

"I have. But I've never come across it."

"You plan to work in Sector 3 in the Seventeenth District, don't you?"

"Yes."

"Then, you won't be able to find fuel for a steam engine there."

"There are some sub-glacial forests being exploited by isolated woodsmen. And, I could import some fuel from the surrounding districts..."

Talking to the Lieutenant, Lien felt that he was facing mysterious opposition from above. A mere Class-2 Glaciologist never had, and never would obtain a much-prized steam engine that would confer on him a simulacrum of freedom and independence. Such things were almost exclusively reserved for the top levels of the Company, Security, Maintenance, the Dispatchers and their wives.

Lieutenant Skoll was making notes in the margin of Lien's application. Then, he sighed.

"Very well. I'll forward your request."

"When can I expect an answer?"

"Probably in a week."

"But I have to leave tomorrow... I'm going on a month-long expedition. It's important..."

"I'm sorry, Glaciologist, but there's nothing more I can do."

Lien left the office. In the anteroom, the meat wholesaler looked at him questioningly, but Lien avoided his eyes. If the man really had sabotaged his loco-car's red box, then he was subject to a year of hard labor in one of the Northern District's labor camps, located in the outer periphery of the Company's territory. Beyond that point, there was only the constantly changing Front of the seemingly everlasting war that the Trans-European Company was waging against its powerful, eastern neighbor, the Siberian Company. Several years ago, Lien had served two years in an armored train that operated as a shuttle between the various Fronts. One day, his train had hit a mine and his right leg had been badly injured.

As a result, he had been discharged and sent back to civilian life.

Lien met Go Farrell, his assistant, at a pre-arranged
meeting place in a cafe near the Security building. When
his friend silently questioned him, he shook his head
negatively.

"We have to wait eight days for an answer, but I
think it'll be no."

"Too bad. You want a beer? Something warm?"

"No. I'll have a vodka."

Farrell then proceeded to rave about a new cabaret
train that had just arrived in Grand Star Station from the
South.

"... And they have girls like you've never seen! I
want to go tonight. It's great! It travels on ten rails, can
you imagine?"

"Which reminds me... I've heard that they're moving an entire town," Lien said. "F Station. It was all over
the grapevine. A hundred thousand people. Three or four
hundred rails, on the Great Northern Network."

"An entire town? All at once? But why?"

Lien drank his vodka down in one gulp and sighed.

"Dissidence. First, the Company cut their power off
to teach them a lesson, but apparently, it wasn't
enough."

"How on Earth could the poor buggers cope without
power?"

"I don't know. They must have burned everything
that they could get their hands on. But in the end, the
Company decided to deport them. That means that tomorrow, traffic on the Great Northern Network will be
blocked until nightfall. But at least they won't go
through here."

When they left the cafe, Lien once again looked up towards the dome. The Redfurs were still there, clearing off the snow.

"You're fascinated by them, aren't you?" said Farrell. "It's not the first time I've caught you looking at them..."

"I don't understand why nobody has ever tried to understand how they can live outside. During the two hundred fifty years of this new ice age, there've only been some minor, insignificant works published about them..."

"They refuse to be studied. When you try to get near them, they take off into the wilderness, where none of our trains can follow. Forget about them. Let's go look at the Seventeenth District Governor's train instead... Fifteen rails, a real palace, full of servants, and beautiful women wearing exotic furs... But we can't get too close, because it's heavily guarded."

As they neared the mobile palace, they noticed a disturbance amongst the crowd. Lien saw a strikingly beautiful, young, blonde woman, enveloped by a white fur coat, walking by looking disdainful. Behind her, two other girls, more simply dressed, obviously her servants, were carrying packages.

"That's Floa Sadon, the Governor's daughter. She must have been out shopping. People say she's naked under all her furs!"

Lien laughed.

"If you believe everything people say..."

"But it's true! Her conductor told me."

A strangely brazen, yet light, wisp of perfume floated behind the girl. Catching a brief whiff of it, a strong wave of depression washed over Lien, leaving him feeling suddenly powerless. But he overcame it, and looked resolutely in front of him.

Farrell was loudly expressing his admiration for the two steam engines that were pulling the Governor's train. They were two steel monsters, almost permanently clouded by powerful jets of steam, a symbol of power and wealth. The mobile palace effectively traveled over fifteen rails. One could have wandered inside as easily as in one of the ancient pre-ice age buildings. Lien fantasized that it contained lush patios and water fountains, all decorated in that rococo and somewhat ridiculous style that the directors of the Company seemed to enjoy. He remembered that, while he was at the Front, a general had had a replica of a Venetian palace built. Because the enormous palace needed twenty rails to travel, sometimes reinforcements had to be postponed or rerouted because it was in transit...

"Did you see those two engines?" asked his assistant. "Six men standing on top of each other couldn't reach the smokestacks. They must have tons of coal and water in there. No wood, obviously. And they have to be able to travel under electric power too, if need be."

Lien estimated that the Governor's mobile palace must have had four floors and about thirty rooms; it required an insane amount of energy to move such a mass on rails. Sometimes, the smaller power substations blew a fuse when a director took a fancy to travel from one end of the Company to the other.

Farrell nudged him with his elbow; at one of the windows of the second floor, the silhouette of a woman was standing still, watching them.

"I bet it's the Sadon girl. Do you think she's noticed us?"

15

"I'm going home to file my notes," Lien said. "Are you coming?"

"No. I'm going to buy us something for dinner. Occasionally one of us has to think about eating."

Lien took one of the commuter shuttles which travelled along the vast, busy network of Grand Star Station. He and Farrell lived in a small train, parked on a minor line, located at the other end of the Station. To get back there on foot would have taken him all day. During the trip, he sometimes turned a distracted glance to the huge, waiting convoys, the armored trains, and the mobile fortresses, all traveling towards the Siberian Front. They said that, in the last few weeks, the fighting had suddenly become fiercer, the two sides battling endlessly for the possession of a small, strategic zone which was crisscrossed by a dozen important rail lines.

Lien and Farrell's train had three cars. They lived in the first, which was also the engine. The second one contained all their equipment and scientific instruments, including a powerful drill which could be used to obtain ice samples, even at very great depths. The last car served as an office, as well as the living quarters of their crew. For the moment, the men were on a leave which would end at midnight. But Lien didn't expect them to be back until morning. And some would probably wait to catch up with the train at a junction, when it stopped at some small, out of the way Station. But now, there was that problem with F Station, the town that the Company was exiling to the Great North, and which was going to jam all traffic along the entire Great Northern Network It must be moving very slowly, Lien thought, not more than six or seven miles per hour. He tried to imagine its anxious citizens, locked in their small living quarters, unable to leave or, even if they could, exist in the merciless cold of the exterior, which would kill them in only a few seconds...

Before entering his office, Lien again looked at the dome which, near the edge of the city, was closer to the surface. A few miles away it met the ice; beyond it was the endless icy wilderness, covered by layers and layers of snow, which fell on an average of one day out of three.

There was a Redfur campsite just near the edge of the dome, and Lien could see wisps of smoke rising from a fire. The Ice People only used fire to cook their food. If their departure was to be postponed because of F Station, Lien decided to go there the following day to meet with the Redfurs. He would have liked to have some of them on his crew, and vaguely felt that their presence would enable him to make important discoveries. But the Company insisted on being the only ones to have any contact with the Ice People. In addition, Lien knew that they would have felt that a Redfur on his crew was undesirable for conducting scientific work.

Instead of filing his notes, as he had told Farrell he intended to do, Lien studied the map of their future worksite. It was located north-east of what was once called Poland, near a town called Bialystok, which now lay buried under millions of tons of ice over half-a-mile thick.

The Company was having some problems with the area; the thickness of the ice there was increasing at a much faster rate than anywhere else. Because of this, heavy work was required to maintain the stability of the lines. Already, the Company had had to build some ice tunnels, which did not please Maintenance. So, the Glaciologist Corps had been given the mission of discovering the cause of the increase in thickness. The former

Polish city was already buried under three thousand feet of ice, whereas elsewhere, the ground was only seven hundred to two thousand feet beneath the surface of the ice. There were even some places in the South where the ice thickness did not exceed one hundred seventy feet. People had dug shafts down to the ground and found old installations from before the ice age. In Southern Germany, for example, there was an ancient forest that was being "mined" by industrious woodsmen.

When the telephone rang, Lien thought that it was Farrell calling to ask about that night's dinner menu.

"This is Governor Sadon's private secretary. His Excellency is giving a reception tonight, and would be happy if you could attend it in your capacity of Glaciologist working in his District. The reception starts at nine. Please wear your dress uniform."

"I'm very flattered but..."

They'd hung up before he had time to explain that his dress uniform was at the cleaners. Furious, Lien slammed his fist on the desk and considered the problem. He had been given no choice, he had to go out again to get that green and black dress uniform. It would have been inconceivable to go to the Governor's reception without it.

As he was leaving, Farrell stepped off a commuter shuttle, his arms full of groceries.

"Wait for me!" Lien shouted to the driver. Then, to Farrell, "I'll be right back. I'll explain everything later."

It wasn't easy getting the dress uniform out of the Company's cleaners. Then, finding another train to get home proved even more difficult. It was rush hour, and commuters fought to get seats on the various express shuttles, which all seemed to arrive simultaneously. Eventually, Lien had to settle for taking an omnibus which travelled around the Station's Periphery, and it took him an hour to get home.

"An invitation from Governor Sadon?" Farrell said after Lien apprised him of the situation. "It's the girl! She saw you before in the crowd and got you an invite."

"You're crazy."

"No. I saw her. She looked at you with her big green eyes and that was enough. Then, she looked at you again from her window."

Lien shrugged and left to clean and iron his uniform, which had barely been processed by the cleaners. In fact, he had all but forgotten about it, since he hadn't worn it for months.

"I hope I haven't put on any weight."

"I can't even lend you mine, because you're taller than me."

"You've got to get me a loco-taxi for eight thirty. Try ordering one by phone.

"Okay. I'll do my best."

Waiting for the loco-taxi, they had a drink. Farrell was smiling enigmatically in a way that irritated Lien.

"Cut it out, will you?"

"You're nervous, I can tell. You're going to see Floa Sadon at that reception. Do you think she's going to be naked under her furs?"

"It's a full dress party. She'll probably be wearing a dress, not her furs."

"So?"

At the palace entrance, Security gave Lien a badge that he had to pin to his uniform. Then, a servant showed him to the end of a long line of people who were all waiting to be introduced to the Governor. Lien waited patiently, looking around. Suddenly, he saw Floa Sadon. She was wearing a long, black dress that went down to her feet, but which bared her entire back down to her buttocks, and covered very little of her chest. She noticed him watching her, and smiled at him provocatively. Then, she walked towards him, but abruptly turned away. Lien could see the voluptuous shape of her buttocks moving beneath the thin black fabric. Suddenly he was flustered, and felt a strong desire for her. At the same time, he smelled a whiff of the same strong, seductive perfume that he had noticed in the afternoon.

"Ah, Lien Rag, Class-2 Glaciologist," the Governor said, muttering through his thick, grey mustache. "I'm glad to see you. I want that ice thickening business solved as soon as possible; I'm counting on you. If you succeed, I can guarantee you a promotion to Class-1."

"Well, the problem is rather complex and..."

But the next person in line had already pushed him out of the way before he could complete his sentence. It was obviously not the right time to give a lecture. He found himself free, alone, and bored, so he decided to go over to the buffet to get a cup of an amber-colored liqueur, obviously made from fruit grown under dome conditions. Then, he took another walk around the party.

"So, you're the Glaciologist?" a mocking voice suddenly said near his shoulder.

Floa Sadon stood behind him, and he could not repress a smile. She took him by the arm and dragged him back to the buffet. There, she filled a plate with various canapés, then pointed towards a low couch set up on a secluded patio, at the center of which was an illuminated fountain. The water changed colors as it fell harmoniously. Lien remembered how, earlier in the afternoon, when he had looked at the exterior of the palace, he had had an intuition about this kind of decor.

"I'm the one who got you invited," Floa said. "My father couldn't care less about the ice sciences."

"I think you're wrong," Lien replied calmly. "Right now, the thickening of the ice in the Bia Sector is one of District Seventeen's most pressing problems."

She shrugged.

"Nevertheless, you weren't included on the guest list."

"Why should I have been? I'm only a Class-2 Glaciologist."

"Let's eat instead of arguing."

Lien didn't know the names of most of what was on his plate, but he knew that they were rare and expensive foods. The caviar, for instance, must have come from sturgeon breeding farms in expensive artificial lakes. There were also filets of caribou tongue, and pastries with surprising and delicate flavors.

"I saw you outside this afternoon, and I felt like meeting you."

Lien shook his head.

"I don't believe you."

She stomped her feet. He then realized that she wasn't wearing shoes. He admired the delicacy of her feet, and suddenly thought of the Redfurs, outside, cleaning the snow-covered dome. At that moment, he could not grasp the meaning of such a thought.

"You don't believe me?"

"No, I don't."

"They haven't told you about me? Haven't you heard that as soon as I see a new man, the only thing I want is to make love to him?"

"No. Nobody told me anything like that."

"Well, your friend seemed eager to meet me," she said petulantly.

Lien tried to appear polite.

"My friend behaves that way with all the pretty girls."

"What about you? Has the study of ice made you equally as cold?"

"No, of course not... But, to be perfectly honest, I feel out of place here. Look over there. That's Professor Elam, my boss. What's he going to think if he sees me here, with you?"

"You're right. Let's get out of here," she said. "Come with me."

She took him by the hand and he discovered that the vast palace still had more surprises in store for him. They took a thickly-carpeted elevator, which deposited them in a plush corridor, leading to the Governor's daughter's room. It was huge and even had a pool.

There, Floa told Lien to sit in a chair while she moved towards the center of the room. Abruptly, she unclasped her dress and stood in front of him, totally naked. Lien remained still, although his heartbeat increased.

The young girl then opened a hidden closet and took out an isothermal suit and a fur coat. She quickly appraised Lien's size at a glance and gave him the suit.

"Put it on."

The isothermal suit fit him like a glove. Lien was surprised.

"Hurry," Floa said impatiently.

"But where are we going?"

"I'll explain later if you don't mind."

Then, she added with a perverse laugh.

"You don't mind getting dressed in front of me, do you?"

CHAPTER TWO

At first, Lien wasn't overly surprised at being taken to a small loco-car owned and operated by Floa. But from the moment they exited the electronically-activated airlock and found themselves outside of the palace, he was amazed to discover that the little vehicle was travelling exclusively on high-priority lines.

"You've got a brown box?" he asked the Governor's daughter.

"A black one," she replied.

He tried to hide his astonishment. How many people could there be with one of the Company's much-prized black boxes? A few hundred? Probably not even that many. There were four kinds of boxes. Red ones, yellow ones, brown ones and black ones. They were used to decode the electronic signals transmitted along the rails and they alone could control the movement of private and public railcars. Someone possessing only a red box had to be resigned to taking a back seat to all other priority travelers. As a result, they would find themselves repeatedly shunted off onto secondary lines, hassled by numerous Security checks, and even told to wait on sidings. Lien Rag's train was equipped with a yellow box, which was just a step higher than a red one. But to have a steam engine, and a black box as well, was to be at the very top of the Company's social ladder.

"I suppose this loco-car belongs to your father," Lien said, with a note of respect creeping into his voice in spite of himself.

"No. It's registered in my name. Why?"

Lien smiled sarcastically.

"I didn't know I was travelling with one of the Company's V.I.P.'s, that's all."

Floa laughed in mild embarrassment.

"I inherited a lot of shares from my mother. That makes me a major stockholder, and comes with all kinds of privileges. Does that answer all your questions?"

Lien preferred not to reply. Instead, he looked out into the distance. The loco-car's single light shone ahead on the rails. They were travelling very close to the far left side of the city's network. Visible to the right were hundreds and hundreds of lines, all gleaming softly in the darkness. They passed many trains, but none passed them. Obviously, at that hour, no one with a higher priority than theirs was travelling on the network.

"Where are we going?" Lien asked.

"To see some friends."

Suddenly, a green light lit up on the instrument panel. Floa took a magnetic card from the glove compartment and slid it into a special slot on the side of the black box. Normally, all the boxes were hermetically sealed. Lien still remembered the fat, meat wholesaler's fear at being accused of having sabotaged his box.

"I'm switching to steam power," she explained.

She obviously was preparing to leave the main network to travel on secondary or possibly even smaller lines. Soon, the characteristic puffing of a steam engine replaced the soft whirring of electric power.

"Isn't it strange that, in order to be free, we should have to revert to steam?" Floa remarked. "Now that the Trans-European network is almost totally electrified, and only a few privileged people like me have access to an autonomous form of energy, it turns out to be something from the past. It's ironic, isn't it? In the past, compared to steam, electricity was considered a sign of progress.

Now, it's the opposite. Ah, I see we're going to leave the main lines... But what are all those lights?"

The view had suddenly become incredibly impressive. To their right, all the rail lines appeared to be occupied by hundreds, perhaps thousands, of trains. It looked like a collection of huge garlands of light illuminating the icy darkness.

"It must be F Station," Lien answered with a harsh tone in his voice. "They're being exiled to the Great North."

"Oh, yes, I've heard about it. I think the Company had some kind of problem there... But isn't the view just wonderful?"

"It depends on who's looking at it. I bet the hundreds of thousands of people who live in F Station aren't too thrilled by it right now."

Suddenly, the loco-car rushed into a deep trench which had only two rail lines. In spite of the narrowness of the passage, Floa showed no signs of slowing down. Lien felt increasingly nervous. At their speed, a chunk of ice on the line could cause a fatal accident. He wondered if the loco-car was equipped with some kind of early warning system.

"Don't worry," Floa said, observing his nervousness. "In spite of its looks, this line is really well maintained. It's only later on that it starts being rough -- when it becomes a single line."

"A single line?"

"Well, what do you expect? It only services an abandoned mine that was closed fifty years ago, and a few isolated farms."

They were lucky that it was no longer snowing. The rails were visible up to three hundred feet ahead. Automatically, the next switch sent them onto a single line track that headed directly into the icy wilderness. Because of the nature of his job, Lien was used to travelling on these almost forgotten, often neglected lines, which were frequently damaged in places. But he had never before found himself on one in the company of a gorgeous girl, especially at breakneck speed!

Like a flash in the night, they passed a small reindeer ranch, illuminated only by a few, meager lights, and a local farm where a few crops of wheat and corn grew under the permanent light of a heating unit. Soon, there was nothing outside to see but the endless ice. The vibrations of the coach indicated a growing distortion of the rails, further proof of the line's disuse. Floa began to slow down, and offered Lien one of the green cigars that had suddenly become very fashionable in Grand Star Station, which he refused.

"In two minutes, we'll be on an old siding," she said. "There's even an abandoned station that's half-buried under the ice. Somehow, in fifty years, it hasn't gotten much thicker around here."

"We still don't quite understand what determines the thickness of the ice."

"Some Redfurs live here, but we don't have to worry about them."

"You know, I've never seen any up close," he said.

"Don't pay any attention to these," she said. "We'll see others later."

"Is there anyone waiting for us at the end of this line?"

"Nobody. We'll have to cope on our own."

The loco-car stopped on the ice-encrusted rails with a screech -- fortunately, the heat from the wheels quickly melted the ice.

"Now we have to go a few hundred feet on foot. Is that okay with you?"

"So that's why you took the isothermal suits," Lien said, a little nervously.

He was careful to be sure that the suit's hood, which had been specially equipped with an air filter and heating system, was hermetically closed. Even so, when he stepped outside the airlock he still experienced the same deadly cold that always chilled him to the bone. They began to walk, their legs sinking into fifteen inches of fresh snow.

Soon, they walked by the old rococo station, where only the roof still stood above the ice. Fifty years earlier, before the Company's network had been totally electrified, there were still many isolated people who had to rely on their own power to connect with the major rail lines. Often, they would use steam engines, or rail sleds pulled by dogs or reindeer. But now, such conveyances were extremely rare, and were even frowned upon. Lien had heard that, in the entire Trans-European territory, such primitive means of transportation were only used by a few very isolated villages of fishermen who lived on the ice shelf which had once been the Baltic Sea.

In spite of his good physical condition, Lien was becoming breathless more rapidly than Floa, who seemed to dance as she walked. Somehow, no matter how hard he tried, she always seemed to be a few feet ahead of him. Finally, he saw a light and the shape of some old buildings in front of him.

"It's the top floor of a building that must have had at least twenty-four stories," Floa said. "My friends have tried to go down to what used to be the ground floor, but the ice is solid as steel from the tenth floor down."

"Your friends? Who are they? Outsiders?"

"What if they are?"

In any event, they must have been outsiders with a taste for the good things in life, Lien thought, because as soon as they stepped out of the airlock, he was struck by the exceedingly warm temperature inside the building. Immediately, Floa removed her suit, revealing that she was dressed only in a very skimpy dress which bared most of her long, slender, and attractive, legs.

"I can't take off my suit. I'm only wearing briefs," Lien said.

"So? They're probably all naked anyway."

Indeed, they were. There were about twenty young men and women, but there were also a few older people; Lien was embarrassed by the sight of an older, naked woman whose breasts dangled down to her waist. Nobody seemed to pay much attention, however. They were all listening attentively to a man who was sitting in a corner of the room. From where he stood, Lien could only see his long red hair. Suddenly, he reacted with surprise, and looked again as if to dispel any doubts which he might have had. It really was one of the Ice People who was speaking to the crowd in a monotone voice.

"He talks... Just like us," Lien whispered to Floa.

The others turned towards him to hush him up, and even Floa frowned.

"Shut up."

"Hunt good one day, but not good another... Yesterday, and day before, good. Very good. Wolves, many wolves..."

The Ice Man raised his hand to indicate the approximate height of the pile of wolf skins that his tribe had gathered.

"But trader still not happy..."

Suddenly, he stood up, and Lien could see that he was entirely naked. His body was covered in an attractive, rust-colored, wooly fur. In his hand, the Ice Man held a silver-grey wolf skin, which he proceeded to show to his audience. It travelled from hand to hand.

"It's a dog skin," Lien told Floa.

"It looks like wolf though."

"A dollar for trader, a dollar for you," the Ice Man explained.

"God! It's worth at least ten dollars on the market," said a girl with dark hair and shiny eyes. She was sitting next to the red-furred man and smiled coyly when she saw his long, dangling organ moving between his muscled thighs.

"How can he stand it in here? I thought they died if they were exposed to heat?" Lien whispered again in Floa's ear.

"They give him drugs. I don't know. Even then, he can't stay long. It's almost over, you'll see."

"Why is he willing to do this, then?"

"Money, of course. But, it wasn't easy. It took them months to get him to come..."

Most of the time, the Redfur tribes fled from men. Lien remembered having seen them leave as soon as he and his team had arrived on a site. He certainly had never seen one from this close.

"Why isn't he cleaning snow from the domes, like the others?"

"Not these. They're hunters. They hunt for skins that they sell to traders."

"But isn't that illegal?"

"I suppose so."

Lien looked around and realized that the place where they were must have once been a comfortable

29

dwelling unit. He remembered that they used to be called 'apartments.' Considering the smallness of their rail habitations, he found this one roomy enough. The floor was covered by a thick carpet, on top of which various furs and skins had been spread. The Ice People must have been selling the products of their hunts to the outsiders for a while. There were even skins from animals that Lien had never seen. Only carnivores had survived the new ice age. Other species, such as the fierce snow rabbits, had mutated into meat eaters, their favorite prey being the rats which, as always, continued to thrive. They had adapted to the new age with relative ease, digging tunnels through the ice to reach man's grain silos in the domed cities.

The Ice Man took a glass from one of the girls and downed its contents in a single gulp. The crowd then bought some of his furs, and he left the room.

After his departure, the atmosphere suddenly became less solemn. Lien had the feeling that all these people felt an almost religious awe in regard to the Ice Man, but that they were in fact glad that he was gone. Floa introduced her guest around the group, and he eventually learned that the little community had been thriving for years, in spite of a variety of ups and downs.

"But the power? Where do you get your power?" he asked several times, before he could finally get an answer.

Lien learned that there was a black market for coal and wood throughout the Trans-European. It was very well organized, and even made use of major rail lines to move its merchandise. He was very surprised.

"It's all based on barter," explained one of the men, who seemed to know what he was talking about. "We're exploiting this building like a mine. We recycle semiprecious metals, like lead and copper, which were commonly used in pre-ice age constructions. The wood paneling from an old door is worth a fortune on the antiques black market."

Floa took him into the next room and showed him a very unusual artifact, kept under a small, protective glass dome.

"They look like ancient flowers."

"They are," she said. "But they're not ancient."

"But growing them is forbidden. It would take too much energy to grow them under the domes."

"These weren't grown under a dome. Not really. They're supposed to have come from a place where there is no ice."

Lien shrugged.

"It's another one of those legends that refuse to die. That one seems to have enjoyed a comeback recently. A few weeks ago, someone showed me a blade a grass that he said had grown near a real stream. But I don't believe in any of those stories. They're made up by dreamers and I think they're dangerous. According to the experts, our ice age is going to last anywhere from another two hundred fifty to five hundred years."

She brought him back into the corridor and, suddenly, snuggled very close to him. She proceeded to kiss him passionately on the mouth, while pressing her hips against his, until she could feel his desire growing against her flesh. Then, teasingly, she moved away from him. He found himself ridiculous and alone, with an obvious erection stretching his briefs. But Floa had not left.

"Have you heard of the Oblique Road?" she asked, suddenly serious.

"Funny. That's the second time today someone's asked me that question," he answered, still trying to hide his embarrassment.

"Who asked you before?"

"Lieutenant Skoll, from Security."

"I know him," she said, troubled. "He's a dangerous man. Do you know anything about it?"

"Not much. I think it's just another legend. A line that crosses the entire Company and leads towards another place, one that's not buried under the ice, but a place where it's possible to live outside, without relying on rails and trains... No, I don't believe in it."

"I've heard that there are some people who did locate the Oblique Road, but that they disappeared and haven't been heard from since. I like to think that they're still alive, somewhere in an iceless land..."

They returned to the other room, where the others were drinking and eating. Lien gathered that Floa had brought some food with her, and that her friends had gone out to her loco-car to get it.

A small, attractive brunette walked up to him. He immediately noticed her firm, naked little breasts, the nipples of which pointed up perkily.

"You're one of Floa's friends, aren't you? What a shame. I live in a commune near here; we came in a rail sled. Lemme guess... I bet you're with Maintenance."

"No, I'm a Glaciologist."

"Not much better," she said. "Do you enjoy fucking one of the Company's shareholders? I don't understand why they let her in here. She likes to play at being an outsider, but in the end, she's always happy to go back to her loco-car and her daddy's palace. I saw it once on the Network. It's a monstrosity. What a circus!"

She put her arm around him and discreetly led him to the other side of the room.

"I like you, you know. My name's Ariel. Do you like me?"

"Ariel? I thought that was a boy's name?"

"So? What makes you think I'm a girl? You haven't looked under my skirt yet!"

Indeed, Lien had been so caught up in peering at Ariel's breasts that he hadn't noticed that she was wearing a very short mini-skirt. But before he could say anything, she laughed, digging her nails into his arms.

"Don't worry, silly! I really am a girl! But what would you say if I told you that I like to fuck Redfurs?"

"That's your business," he replied curtly.

"My, my, aren't we a prude! Do you think it's disgusting, like doing it with animals? You know, they're better hung than all of the rest of you living in your goddamn domes. Somebody told me that sexual potency has been decreasing ever since the new ice age began."

"I doubt that," he said.

He didn't particularly wish to provoke her, nor did he care for the turn of conversation. He didn't approve of women, outsiders or not, who spoke so crudely about sex, any more than he approved of locker room talk between men.

"But I don't think you have anything to worry about," she continued, suddenly all sweetness and smiles again. "I saw you earlier when you came back with Floa. Your briefs looked quite, er, full..."

"Excuse me," he said, and began to walk away.

"No, wait," she begged. "If you want, you can join my commune. Do you really want to go back to Grand Star Station? Are you in love with Floa? Is that it? You do know that she's frigid, don't you?"

He finally succeeded in getting away from her and went back to get a drink from a barrel that was sitting on a table. It was a rather strong, fruity wine, with a pleasant taste.

"I see that you scored a hit with Ariel," said Floa's ironic voice from behind his back. "If you want to fuck her, feel free. I'll wait. I'm not going to abandon you here, a hundred twenty miles from Grand Star Station."

"One hundred twenty miles?" he said, genuinely astonished. "But it didn't even take us an hour to get here."

"I was driving fast," she replied.

"Are we going to stay long?"

"Do you want to leave?"

She looked at a small watch that was grafted directly onto her wrist and was powered by her nerve impulses.

"You're right," she said finally. "It's pointless to stay."

"Why did we come then?"

But she preferred not to answer. A small group of outsiders accompanied them to Floa's loco-car. That was the least they could do, considering how much merchandise she had brought with her, Lien thought. He had estimated that it was worth more than three times his monthly income.

When they were back in the car, alone, travelling along the single rail line, he decided to again ask her about the reason for their escapade.

"You're repeating yourself," she said sullenly.

Suddenly, the loco-car stopped dead in its tracks, in the middle of the icy wasteland. Lien became terrified at the thought that a malfunction could strand them there, on the half-forgotten line, for hours. Before they could be rescued their power source would surely run out, and then they would die.

"Come with me," Floa said.

"You stopped on purpose?" he asked, relieved.

She went into the back compartment of the loco-car, which had been richly furnished and turned into a small, but cozy cabin. She began to take off her clothes.

"I want to make love to you. Now," she said sarcastically. "Isn't that a good enough reason for you?"

Lying naked on a low couch, she opened her arms invitingly. During their lovemaking, she seemed to enjoy his performance. But, at the back of Lien's mind were the perfidious remarks that Ariel had uttered earlier. It didn't stop him from enjoying himself, but he couldn't help wondering if Floa wasn't just faking it.

Their return journey was made mostly in mutual silence. When they got back onto the network, they saw the lights of F Station again. At six or seven miles per hour, the town would take its time going north.

"Do you think they're really unhappy?" Floa asked. "Maybe some of them are making love right this minute, to take their minds off their problems."

"I don't know. They must be really scared."

"But then, why did they rebel against the Company? It's absurd in the world we live in."

"It's easy for you to say that," he said. "For you, life in the ice age has been spent in the greatest comfort. But they're condemned to spend their whole miserable existence surviving in mobile warrens. They have no loco-cars, not even the ones with red boxes. They can't go anywhere."

"Don't get carried away. If they want to travel, they can take public transportation."

"To go where? To other stations, as ugly as theirs?"

She shrugged.

"You seem to have become a bit of a rebel yourself. Is it because of hanging around with that Ariel girl?"

"I only saw her for a couple of minutes."

"Did she tell you that she fucks Redfurs because they've got big pricks?"

"I don't like to talk about that kind of thing."

"Why? Do you find it disgusting, or maybe it excites you? Would you like to do it to a Redfur girl?"

"Please."

"Some of them are very cute, you know, even with their fur. Or maybe, it's because of their fur. It must be soft, hmm?"

He ignored her. For the first time in his life, he was watching a rather unusual spectacle. Several armored trains and one impressive mobile fortress had been forced to stop to let Floa's little loco-car pass by. The privileges of priority, he reflected. She noticed his amazement and laughed.

"That might delay the war by a few minutes. Who knows, I might have saved some people who would have otherwise died."

"Or doomed them."

"Why are you so negative. You're extremely unpleasant --but a good lover."

"How would you know?"

He immediately regretted his words. Floa had turned livid and looked at him with something close to hate in her face.

"Did that bitch Ariel tell you that I was frigid?"

"Are you?"

"I don't have to tell you. It's none of your fucking business. Think what you want."

He thought that she would take him back to the Governor's palace, but instead, she dropped him off not too far from his train.

"Thank you," he said. "I'll return the suit tomorrow. Could you have my uniform sent back?"

"Certainly," she said rather curtly.

She let him off without a second glance, and left immediately. Lien entered the first car and walked towards his cabin. Just then, Farrell's cabin opened and a tall, strikingly beautiful, naked brunette walked out.

"Sorry," she said, smiling.

She walked past him, going towards the bathroom. He followed her shapely buttocks with his eyes as she went by, and was suddenly struck by the presence of silver sequins stuck to the girl's skin. Was his assistant into a heretofore unrevealed perversion?

He decided to wait for her to return to find out the truth.

"What's all that stuff?" he asked her, pointing at the sequins.

"I'm an exotic dancer at the Cabaret Mikki," she replied. "You must be Lien Rag. Go told me about you."

She held her hand out and he shook it. Suddenly, he was struck by the humor of the situation. There he was, in his own train, at three in the morning, shaking hands with a naked, silver-covered exotic dancer.

CHAPTER THREE

It was eight o'clock and most of the members of the glaciological team had arrived, but the departure clearance had not. Lien had woken up feeling hung over. He kept turning the previous night's events over in his mind; in his sleep, he had tried to solve the mystery of Floa's strange behavior.

Farrell joined him. He had black, puffy circles under his eyes and his speech was slurred.

"I saw your little dancer, last night," Lien said. "She was walking through our loco-car, naked..."

"Yeuse? She's a terrific girl. She's still in bed, I'm getting her breakfast. Do you think we'll be able to leave soon?"

"F Station must still be jamming the Great Northern Network. What difference does it make, anyway? In less than two hours, we'll have caught up with it, and we'll only have to wait again."

"You know what I heard? They're saying that F Station is really a concentration camp that they're moving near the Front to scare the soldiers. Supposedly there were several mutinies in a mobile fortress and in an armored train..."

"A concentration camp..." Lien repeated, rubbing his head.

Not long after, they received the call from Security; Lien was to report to Lieutenant Skoll immediately. He thought anxiously of his nocturnal escapade.

"I may have a little problem," he told Farrell. "I met some outsiders last night. And a Redfur."

"Give me a break! I can take the outsiders, but the Redfur, no way! You've got to be joking."

"I wish. I better see what Skoll wants."

As soon as Lien entered the room, the small, Asian man took off his glasses and began wiping them.

"I've got good news for you, Glaciologist Rag. You've just been approved for use of an LB 117 steam car, one of the latest models. It works with any kind of fuel, even reindeer chips if you're stuck in any isolated areas. We'll give you vouchers for wood and coal, however, use them sparingly and don't lose them. They're worth a lot on the black market. If we find out that you've sold them, you'll be heavily fined. Here's the permit for the loco-car. Pick it up at sub-station 71Q. And take a mechanic with you, because we won't accept any complaints later on."

"This is great news, Lieutenant, thank you," Lien said, too happy to believe what he was hearing, and unable to think of anything else to say.

Skoll watched him, smiling a bit scornfully.

"Don't thank me, Glaciologist. You owe this to a special request by the Governor himself. His Excellency insisted that you be given this loco-car. You're quite privileged. Anyway, you'll still only have a yellow box."

"What's the LB 117's autonomy?"

"Twenty-four hours at medium speed," answered Skoll sharply.

As Lien was heading towards the door, Skoll called him back.

"Just another minute of your time. I know where you were last night. You shouldn't hang around with people like that, Glaciologist. They're parasites, black marketers."

"Going there wasn't my idea," Lien replied.

"During your conversation with them, did anyone happen to mention the Oblique Road?"

Lien shook his head, and Skoll let him go. He was so happy that he immediately stopped to call Farrell to tell him the news.

"Send Lamont to 71Q. He knows steam engines. I'll meet him there."

"I'll be there too. I want to see our new wonder."

Lien took a shuttle to the stop for Governor Sadon's palace, hoping to be able to thank him, but the only thing he found was empty rails. According to a local mechanic, the Governor's palace had left Grand Star Station at dawn.

"His Excellency went back to his District," the man explained.

"At dawn?"

"Five a.m. sharp."

But then, how could have Lieutenant Skoll have been advised of the Governor's wishes? Obviously, Floa had pulled some strings. And how did she know that he wanted a steam-powered loco-car?

"Hey, do you need another lift?" the driver of the shuttle asked.

"Yeah. Take me to sub-station 71Q."

When Lien arrived, Lamont was inspecting the underside of the LB 117, which Farrell, a huge grin across his face, was patting as if it was alive. When he saw Lien, he ran over and hugged him.

"I didn't do anything," Lien said. "It's a miracle."

"It's the Sadon girl, isn't it? You must have scored a big hit with her."

"Don't get carried away."

Lamont appeared from beneath the locomotive. His hands were full of grease, but his face was beaming.

"It's a brand new engine," he said. "They didn't give you one of those recycled jobs. We should be able to get some real speed out of her. There's a new turbine for the two front wheels, and a modern furnace that hardly needs any water. She's at full pressure as soon as she's turned on."

Lien took care of the last of the paperwork then ordered a full load of liquid coal. This was extracted by injecting mineral oil under high pressure into the old, sub-glacial mines.

Finally, the three of them boarded the new machine, as happy as little boys.

"I've got such an incredible sense of freedom," Farrell said.

"Don't forget that we still only have a yellow box," Lamont reminded him, being realistic. "That means we have to stop at all the signals."

"Only on the networks," interjected Lien. "We can use any of the secondary lines that we want."

Yeuse, the dancer, was still there when, in front of the entire team, they attached the train to their new engine. She was wearing only ordinary clothes, but Lien was once more struck by her beauty. She had a few unexpected wrinkles at the corners of her eyes, which made her look even more beautiful. There was also a seriousness and gravity to her expression that provided a sharp contrast to the lifestyle she led.

"I've got to go," she said. "Cabaret Mikki is leaving Grand Star Station today for the Seventeenth District. We're going to spend a few weeks in a huge sub-glacial timber factory."

"I know the place," Lien said. "It's the Forest of Ots, I think the original Polish name was Otsztyn. It's huge..."

They had dug fourteen hundred feet under the ice and excavated huge galleries. The timber workers made money hand over fist, which they spent in much the same way.

Lien was sorry to see the girl go, and suddenly he was annoyed that Farrell had met her first.

Later on, Farrel said, "She's a nice girl, but not as much fun as I thought she would be."

That afternoon, they finally received their authorization to leave Grand Star Station, but were asked not to exceed a speed of twenty-five miles per hour.

"That's okay. It'll give us a chance to break in the new engine," Lamont said, but Farrell still scowled at the order.

Precisely at three o'clock, they exited the Security airlock, then the main airlocks which formed a buffer between the Station's comfortable 60 degrees Fahrenheit, and the exterior temperature of minus 60 degrees. Once outside, they had to increase the output of the heating system, and keep careful watch over the new machine's controls.

Further on, the South-West Network joined up with the Great Northern Network, and they came upon traces of F Station's transit. A city of one hundred thousand people leaves obvious signs of its passage when its sewers and garbage are unceremoniously dumped onto the rails.

"It's going to take a pretty big snowfall to cover all of that," Farrell said, his face twisted in disgust.

"The Ice People will take care of it," remarked Lamont, pointing to some fur-covered shapes in the mist. "If they aren't more careful, they're going to get run over."

Lien turned to keep the Redfurs in sight. What could they possibly find in the city's garbage that they could eat? He realized he knew nothing of their way of life, of what they ate. The Company gave food to the ones who cleaned the domes, but what kind of food?

Suddenly, without warning, they were shunted off to a siding. They were stuck in an immense traffic jam, right behind a huge merchandise train. They called the train master on their radio telephone.

"We've been here since eight o'clock," he said. "It's that damn F Station. Looks like we're going to be stuck here all night."

"What are you carrying?" the ever-curious Farrell inquired.

"Synthetic fibers, wool bales and radioactive waste."

"Too bad there's nothing there to drink. Well, then I'm going to go take a nap. I didn't get much sleep last night."

Lien went into his office to try to work, but his mind kept wandering. On a piece of paper, he tried to write down a chronological sequence of the events of the last two days. Once in awhile he looked outside; it had started to snow again. Priority trains passed by frequently, moving at great speeds. Some of them were troop transports and armored convoys. There were rumors that the Company was manufacturing these at the rate of two per day. At the Front, every line was the target of fierce fighting. It wasn't unusual for the two warring Companies to simply launch two armored trains directly at each other. They would crash and explode, and the men who survived were expected to continue to fight in the snow. Then, if thirty feet of line had been gained, the Company issued a triumphant press release. He tried to remember how many rail companies shared the planet, but couldn't. There was the Trans-European, and the Siberian, and the Pan-American, and the African, and in Australasia there were just too many of them to count.

When dinner was ready, everyone ate together except for Farrell, who stayed listening to the traffic updates, which were provided at regular intervals. So far, the yellow box had obstinately remained silent. When their clearance was granted, it would beep and display a signal.

One of the men said, "The last town they moved was Iron Station. They needed miners to go down more than two and a half miles. It was crazy, because the ice pit was completely unstable. The galleries kept getting blocked up by avalanches. All the mining was causing sudden temperature changes. When the miners went on strike, they were all deported to a concentration camp."

"That's what they say F Station's like now," Lien said reluctantly.

"Could be."

"Do you think that a camp of a hundred thousand people could really exist?" he said with horror.

No one answered.

He took a tray of food to Farrell, who still kept watch next to the yellow box. Lien told him he would replace him at midnight.

But, when he woke up, they were again moving, although slowly. He went to the control room where his assistant was with Lamont, who was so excited by the new machine that he couldn't sleep and preferred to drive.

"In twenty minutes, we'll be at the junction we were looking for. From there we'll head towards Bia. If there are no more problems, we should arrive by dawn."

The snow was still falling; large flakes struck the windshield with surprising force. In fact, because of the low temperature, it was really ice. But they still referred to it as snow, like in the ancient times, when it was a sign of the temperature rising. The temperature still rose, but very rarely reached above minus 40 degrees Fahrenheit.

Lien stayed in the engine's cab with Lamont. He could have gone back to bed, but he no longer felt tired and preferred to stay.

"More signs of F Station?"

"Lots. We'll be seeing garbage for miles and miles. Now it'll all get covered in ice."

They arrived at the junction. Lien heard the loud clang of the automatic switch, then, they were travelling on Secondary Line 34 towards the small town of Cross Station.

"We don't have to go through it, we can just go around if you want," Lamont said.

"No. Let's stop. It'll be a good opportunity for checking our supplies."

When they arrived at Cross Station it was four a.m. The old town was covered by a dome that looked more like a gothic canopy than a smooth, modern dome. The airlock doors creaked, and they had to wait ten minutes for the inner door to open.

"They're keeping the temperature at 50 degrees," explained Lamont, who was reading a tattered copy of the "Official Rail Guide/" The book that was like a bible to all travelers. "Not enough energy. It's a meeting place for reindeer breeders and corn growers. Kind of a small market town."

In spite of the early hour, the town bristled with activity. Whole trains of livestock were forming, and they saw lines of reindeer reticently crossing the rail lines, only to be herded into boxcars. Some people were picking up the animals' excrement which, once dried, made a very acceptable fuel. While it was possible to power small vehicles with it, it would probably be used for heating.

Lien went out amongst the breeders and farmers to have a cup of vodka-laced tea. Then, he heartily ate a reindeer meat sandwich while he listened to the conversations around him. The main subject was the price of reindeer meat, not the war. He thought of the surprise reaction he would create if he mentioned the town that was being exiled to the north. No one would have believed him. Security agents were discreet in this type of town. He looked up towards the dome, but the thickness of the ice prevented him from seeing if there were any Ice People working on it.

He was standing at the end of the bar when someone touched him on the elbow. He thought it was Farrell, coming to join him. But when he turned, he saw a young man with long brown hair and a strange, vacant look.

"Are you with the steam loco, Voyager?"

Lien nodded, as he continued to eat his sandwich.

"Do you have any fuel vouchers for sale?"

This time, Lien shook his head negatively.

"I'll give you a hundred dollars, Voyager."

"Sorry."

"Okay, I see you weren't born yesterday. You know the going rate; two hundred."

It was as much as he made in a month. He looked at the young man again, and thought he looked pleasant enough, but he wanted to end this type of discussion.

"Listen, I don't mind buying you a drink, but I'd rather change the subject."

"You can use the Company's power to recharge your batteries. No one'll know that you sold any vouchers. Two fifty."

"No, I can't. You'll have to find someone else."

"There's no one else using a steam engine in Cross Station, except for Security. Last year, one of their captains was selling his vouchers, but he got caught and replaced."

Lien shrugged, indicating that he had no intention of facing the same fate as the unfortunate captain.

"Okay," the long-haired man said finally. "Do you have anything else to sell?"

"No; sorry."

"What! But you have a ton of supplies. I checked. I'm looking for tea, bread, flour. I'll take anything."

"Forget it, kid. And some guys who look like Security just came in. Be careful."

The young man immediately walked away discreetly, and Lien was able to finish his sandwich in peace. He looked at the busy traffic. Reindeer were herded out of the breeders' trains and into the traders' in what seemed to be an endless cycle. He ordered a beer, and asked the waiter if that was the case.

"Only until noon. Later, it'll be the corn growers. But you can have fun here too, if you want."

Discreetly he handed Lien a card on which a naked couple performed various sexual acts; on it was an address.

"It's not too far from here. Line 51. Very discreet. Only ten dollars."

"Thanks," Lien answered, pocketing the card.

He finished his beer slowly and went back to the loco-car, where Farrell was just getting up. Lamont had finished taking the inventory of their supplies and was checking a list of what they needed.

"I'm going shopping," he said to Lien. "Is there any place you'd suggest?"

"It seems like an okay town. They even have a whorehouse."

"I'm not surprised with all those traders' pockets full of dough. It's not very warm here; they must have a problem getting enough power."

A few hours later they were ready to leave. The new day had arrived, with its pale, dim light. After exiting Cross Station's airlock, they drove past an endless series of domed train-barns full of reindeer. The animals spent most of their lives there, providing milk, food and leather. Occasionally, they saw a domed corn plantation. One of these farms could feed several train-barns. Then, signs of life became scarcer.

"We're going to have to look for the right switch," Farrell said. "And it's not going to be easy, because the automatic signal doesn't seem to be working."

"If the signal at Mark 113 works, then we'll be okay," Lien replied, looking at the Guide. "It's exactly ten miles from the switch. Let's hope our odometer is right and we won't have to get out and walk in the snow."

But the Guide was inaccurate, and they found the old, almost-forgotten line they were looking for, almost three thousand yards ahead of where it should have started. It was listed in the Guide as S 68; it began between two cliff-like ice blocks and ran parallel to the main line, but from the opposite direction.

"I didn't think it would run like that, we'll be going in the wrong direction," Farrell said. "Should we travel in reverse?"

"Why? We'll be the only ones on it."

But the automatic switch refused to work and they had to go outside to unfreeze it. It took two men with a blowtorch to restore it completely, then, Farrell cautiously drove their train onto the old line, where it looked like no other vehicle had been for many years.

"We'll be lucky if we don't have to burn ten feet of ice off the rails up ahead."

The Company had always refused to give them the laser tools that could melt mountains of ice in mere minutes, so they had to use old-fashioned fuel burners. They drove on for several yards then Farrell stopped.

"I'd better go and take a look," he said. "I'm glad I kept my isothermal suit on."

He was out for almost five minutes then returned looking preoccupied.

"What's the matter?"

"I had a hunch. The switch was frozen because somebody who was here before us unstuck it with boiling water. It's a stupid way to do it, because afterwards, it refreezes even harder. Anyway, that means there's probably another car in front of us. A small autonomous unit, I'd guess."

"Steam-powered?"

"I don't know."

But they reached the Bia Sector without seeing any other vehicles, and Lien thought his friend had been overly suspicious.

"Today we'll take some measurements," Lien told the team. "Tomorrow we'll start building a temporary line to take us a couple of hundred yards from here. I think that should be enough for our drilling."

He raised his head and looked in the direction he was indicating when, suddenly, he saw the Ice Man, five hundred yards away. He found himself speechless, and signaled to Farrell to look through the double-glazed windows.

"I don't see anything," his assistant said.

"It's impossible. He was right there. They must have a campsite nearby."

"In general, they like staying near the cities."

"But they hunt too. Wolves and other snow creatures."

Farrell looked at him suspiciously.

"How do you know that? Have you suddenly become an expert on Redfurs?"

"I know, that's all," Lien answered, annoyed.

"Well, he's not there anymore," Farrell said.

CHAPTER FOUR

Lien was sleeping soundly when someone banged loudly on his door. He woke up and took a few seconds to remember where he was, and then he heard Farrell's voice.

"Come out here, quick!"

He hurriedly put on his clothes and ran out into the corridor; Farrell was in the small dining-room.

"Yann's the one who saw them. He was getting ready to place some explosive charges for our seismic tests..."

"Wolves. There are dozens of wolves!"

"Dozens? Don't make me laugh! I counted over a hundred. And I get a funny feeling, like they're going to attack us."

They had been working at the Bia Sector for three days. The day before they had finished installing eight hundred feet of new tracks with a temporary switch, so that it would be possible for any other trains to pass them, although this was a rarely travelled line. But Lien liked to obey the Company's rules, which required such installations in situations like theirs.

"You're the one who thought that somebody else came through here before us," Lien had told Farrell, when the latter had argued that installing the temporary line was a waste of their time. "There could be isolated farms, or even outsiders living around here. We can't block the only line. And once we start drilling, we're not going to be able to move that easily. It would take a day to take the drill apart and reassemble it. So, we don't have any choice."

He went to look at the wolves. They were huge. He had never seen animals of that size, even in zoos. They must have been direct descendants of the wolves that lived in the Polish forests before the ice age. By creating panic amongst the human race, the lower temperatures had been favorable to their species. They had become the major predators of this new age. At least the most common ones, since there were also ice tigers, ice grizzlies and even some mythical animals called "were-beasts," which no one had ever actually seen. Of course, it was only a legend, but one that remained hard to debunk.

Thinking about the way that various creatures had adapted to the incredibly low temperatures, Lien once more turned his mind to the Ice People...

"They're surrounding us," Farrell said, interrupting his reverie.

The entire team had met in the little dining-room, which had windows on both sides of the car. The wolves were indeed beginning to encircle the train. Some were sitting patiently, others were pacing. They were all shiny, grey, and almost six feet high.

"They don't look particularly hungry."

Yann, the seismologist, explained how he had gotten up before dawn to go out and place his explosive charges at strategic locations around the train. The first thing he had seen was glowing points in the icy night.

"I never thought it could be something like those animals' eyes," he explained, still feeling shaken. "Then, I smelled something through my air filters. It was disgusting, the smell of carrion, rotting meat. They stink of it. I didn't think I'd make it back to the train in time, they were so fast. I slammed the airlock right into the jaws of one of them."

"There's got to be more than a hundred of them," another technician said. "I don't ever remember hearing about so many in one place before."

"Okay," Lien said, "let's not panic. Right now they can't hurt us. So we'll do whatever work we can inside the train. Who knows, maybe they'll just get bored and go away."

The team members tried to do as Lien suggested, but every time they looked outside the wolves were still there, waiting patiently.

By noon, everyone was clearly nervous, even Lien. The atmosphere during lunch was tense. Finally, Yann couldn't take it anymore; he stood up violently.

"Listen, we've still got some explosives. Why don't I throw some at them? Either they'll be blown to bits, or run like hell. Why just sit here like saps?"

"Why should we waste valuable supplies? They'll go away eventually. They'll have to."

"I don't know, I have the feeling they're not going to," someone else said. "What we need is a weapon."

"Could we use the flame-throwers?"

"We've got work to do. The only thing that really matters is the drilling. To hell with the wolves."

Finally, nothing was really solved. In the afternoon, Farrell asked Lien to accompany him to the control room. He pointed out the darkening landscape and the wolves, which were still waiting patiently.

"I've been watching them, and I don't think they're here of their own free will."

"What do you mean?"

"I mean that some of them have tried to leave, but they've come back, like there was something or some-one that forced them."

"You're crazy!"

"No, I'd swear it. Look at them. They seem well fed. They have no reason to besiege us like this. I think someone is trying to keep us penned in."

"You sure you haven't been hitting the vodka a little too hard lately?"

Farrell looked offended, but Lien patted him on the shoulder to apologize.

"Let's forget about it for the time being. We have work to do. Why don't we go put that drill together?"

"We still have equipment waiting for us back at Cross Station. When do you want to go back and pick it up?"

"We won't be able to do it tomorrow. The day after, I suppose."

They were talking about a set of ultra-modern drill bits that the Company had had delivered to Cross Station especially for them.

"Why do you want to know?" Lien asked.

"Because I can't help wondering what the wolves will do when we try to leave."

"What can they do? They sure can't prevent us from going. If they try to stop the train, they'll be crushed, that's all."

Farrell didn't seem completely convinced.

They worked on the assembly of the drill until late then they had dinner. From time to time, somebody would turn on the outside lights and a myriad of small glowing points would become visible in the night.

"They're still out there."

Lien asked himself how long some of his teammates' nerves would last. He knew them all well and they had already gone through some incredible adventures together. He remembered the time their drill had burst a natural gas pocket, which was located in an abandoned, pre-ice age mine. They had almost been burned alive, yet everyone had calmly worked together to evacuate the drill car. Another time they had climbed down into a three thousand foot chasm. It had taken them three days to reach the bottom, where they had discovered an unmentionable grave, filled with the corpses of animals and Ice People who had accidentally fallen into it. They had also worked at the Front, on sabotage missions for the Company. Never, in any of these hair-raising situations, had anyone lost his calm. Yet now, the wolves were creating a feeling of panic, simply because they summoned up long-buried ancestral fears.

To enable their work to continue uninterrupted, Lien had broken the team into three shifts that worked day and night. He decided not to go to bed, and to try to last as long as he could, afraid that the crew's highly nervous state might cause an accident. He kept a particular eye on Yann, in case the latter decided to disobey his orders and go out into the night to blast the wolves with explosives. He had also carefully locked away the flame-throwers.

In spite of all Lien's precautions, however, Yann did manage to slip ou unnoticed; taking a powerful portable spotlight, he went outside. By sheer luck, one of the men working near the airlocks noticed the telling drop in temperature, an unmistakable sign that someone had gone outside.

They alerted Lien and began to search the darkness for the seismologist. Almost immediately they found him, shining his light at the wolves. Lien hastily put on an isothermal suit and went outside. In spite of it, as usual, he was seized by the brutal cold. At night, the temperature sometimes dropped to minus one hundred and ten!

"Yann!" he shouted. But the protective hood and air filters muffled his voice.

He saw Yann throw something at the beasts, almost certainly a jury-rigged grenade. At the same time, a crawling shape zeroed in on him. A she-wolf had snuck up behind the seismologist to attack him from the rear.

By chance, another technician had come out with a blowtorch. He had set it so that the flame could reach as far as possible. When the wolf jumped on Yann, he set her on fire from behind. At first she appeared to crumple, then she made an incredible jump, releasing the seismologist. His isothermal suit, which had been pierced by the wolf's claws, let the hot air escape in tiny streams of vapor that instantly turned to ice. The technician kept the wolves at bay with the blowtorch, while Yann, who had come out of his trance, ran back towards the train. Other technicians came out to help Lien pull the blowtorch wielding technician, who also seemed frantically obsessed, back to the train.

Later, they held a meeting for the entire team, even those who had been sleeping, but had been awakened by all the commotion. Lien sipped a cup of vodka-laced tea, as he thought about their next move.

"The wolves are outside for an unknown reason," he said. "We believe it's a kind of attack directed against us."

"Sure. They want to eat us," someone said.

"No, they're well fed. There's got to be something else."

"What? A game of cards maybe?"

A tense laugh rippled through the team. Lien shook his head.

"We don't know. Maybe there's something in our train that's attracting them. A smell, an ultrasonic noise... We should look in that direction."

"I don't think so," Farrell said. "My own opinion is that the wolves are here because they can't leave."

Lien sighed, annoyed that his friend would contradict him publicly. He tried to remain calm.

"You've already told me that you think they're stuck between us and some kind of unknown danger outside their circle. Okay, let's try to find out whether that's the case."

"We've always believed that they're the most dangerous predators, but I'm sure there's much worse. The legends may not be as stupid as you think. Since the ice age there are a lot of incredible new creatures that have surfaced."

"Incredible new creatures?" Lien said calmly, but with obvious skepticism.

"Well, there are the Redfurs, for one. How come no one knows where they come from, or how they can live outside? They're naked at minus sixty, and even their breath doesn't create any vapor."

"Their metabolism is different, that's all," Lien said. It's an adaptation."

"That's easy to say. I heard that, when they were first spotted a century ago, they caused a panic. People thought they were going to attack the domes, destroy them, then pillage and loot the trains. No one knows why they waited a hundred and fifty years after the beginning of the new ice age to show up; but if they did, wouldn't other beasts, even more incredible or more intelligent, wait longer?..."

Farrell helped himself to more vodka and stared at Lien, almost defying him to shut him up.

"I know what I'm talking about. Two years ago, they killed one of those creatures, the ones they call were-beasts. It was ten feet tall and had the body of a bear, and human hands. I saw it."

"Yeah, stuffed, in an amusement park?" Lien replied, immediately regretting his irony.

"No. It was in a hunter's lodge in the Northern District. He kept it locked up, and almost never showed it to anyone. The thing had attacked him, and he'd shot it himself."

"Well, maybe, but let's get back to the wolves. I think that tomorrow we should use the steam engine to head back to Cross Station. We'll cross their circle and see if there really is something that keeps them there, or if they're just attracted to us by something, okay?"

The team muttered their agreement, and even Farrell nodded strongly.

"Are we all going in the steam engine?"

"Except for the security team. We'll need volunteers to keep an eye on the equipment."

No one rushed to volunteer.

"We'll talk about it tomorrow at breakfast," Lien said, rather curtly. "Now, I want everybody either to get back to work or go to their cabins. And I want the outside shutters to stay closed until dawn."

He had not used such a commanding tone of voice in a long time and they were all impressed in spite of themselves. There were no other incidents until dawn.

As usual, the day was slow in coming. Ever since the Moon had exploded, creating an impenetrable cloud of dust around the Earth and blocking the sun's rays, it had been like that. History books said that Earth's satellite had exploded two hundred fifty years before and since then the sun had been totally invisible. There were only a series of bleak days followed by impenetrable nights, both dominated by overpowering cold.

Lien, who had always been interested in history, remembered what he had read. The Moon had been turned into a cosmic garbage bin for atomic waste, until a critical mass of plutonium had been reached and it had exploded. His most treasured possession was a collection of old postcards, now illegal, picturing sunrises and sunsets taken at different locations on the planet: the Mediterranean Ocean, now a solid ice shelf; icy mountain peaks that were themselves now buried under more ice. Two hundred fifty years later these images almost brought tears to his eyes. He understood why the Companies tried so hard to stamp out and erase any memories of what life must have really been like in the ancient times. Even the word "sun" had almost disappeared from the language.

He remembered that, when he was ten, a comet had crossed the cosmic debris surrounding Earth and, for a few minutes, the sky had almost cleared. Thousands of people had been almost blinded by the light. Under the rays of the sun the ice had begun to melt for only two or three hundred seconds, yet it had still provoked untold damage. He had almost missed this incredible experience because his friends, playing a cruel game, had locked him up in a cupboard. The Companies had made sure no pictures of the miraculous event had ever appeared, or were ever again even been mentioned.

The next morning, three men were designated as volunteers to stay behind. Yann, who was feeling very contrite about his behavior of the previous night, was one of them. The rest of the team gathered in the steam engine, which was under Lamont's control. The locomotive was electronically disengaged from the rest of the train and started to move slowly.

Three wolves that had been sitting on the rails raised their noses and moved away just in time.

"Too bad," muttered Lamont between clenched teeth. "I would have enjoyed running them over."

He caught Lien's disapproving look. The Glaciologist didn't much care for that kind of emotional outburst.

"What do we do if the switch won't work?" asked Farrell. "We can't go out to fix it."

"We won't have to," Lien reassured him. "I took a plasma lance."

Lamont slowed down further as they reached the switch, sending it a radio signal; but it refused to work.

"Stop!" Lien shouted.

"We can get closer if you want," replied Lamont.

But suddenly, he understood Lien's agitation; the rails which, only a few days ago, they had installed to link up with S 68 were no longer there. Their engine was barely thirty feet from a clean break in the line. Everything was gone: the rails, the ties, and even the switch itself.

"Am I dreaming or what?"

"No you're not dreaming," said Lien. "It's all gone."

"But they aren't!" pointed out Farrell.

A dozen huge wolves had just appeared from between the snowdrifts.

"Look at them! Their ribs are showing beneath their skin, and they're frothing at the mouth."

Lien admitted that they were hideous-looking. They were different from the others, which had been relatively well-fed and peaceful. These were impatient killers, with bloodlust in their eyes.

"It's out of the question for us to go out to look at the line," said Farrell. "Besides, what is there to see? Someone stole a hundred feet of rails and our switch. It must have weighed a ton. It was probably easy enough to take it apart, but carting it away... You see, I told you someone sent the wolves to keep us here. While we were stuck, they sabotaged the line."

Lamont reclined in his seat and asked softly.

"How long can we keep on producing our own power?"

Lien thought the question was worth asking, but didn't want to talk about it amongst just the three of them.

"Do you really think this is the time to take stock of things?" he asked loudly. "Let's go back to the train and hold a meeting."

"A general meeting?"

"Of course."

They were only a few hundred yards from the train, so it didn't take them long. The three men that had been left behind must have been anxiously watching their unexpected return and wondered what could have caused it.

Lien thought they had a two days' supply of liquid coal and another days worth of batteries; that is, if they made it last as long as humanly possible. He had always planned to go back to Cross Station the next day to get additional fuel, as well as the new drill bits. The drilling alone would have consumed dozens of kilowatts per hour.

Once more they gathered in the dining room. This time, Lien had to force himself to break the heavy silence that greeted him.

"I'm forced to admit that we're facing an unknown enemy who is deliberately trying to prevent us from returning to the main line. We could try to reestablish a temporary connection, but without weapons it will be hard to fight off the wolves. We need to put our heads together to figure out how to keep them away, at least while we're effecting the repairs."

"What about radioing for help?" Yann asked.

"I don't think we should, at least not yet. Our situation isn't totally desperate, and you know how Security feels about using the radio, especially with the war going on. Our standard instructions are to cope on our own."

"Yeah, but if we wait until the last minute to use the radio, it'll be too late," replied Yann. "In the best of cases, it'll take them two days to get here, and we'll all be frozen by then."

"Let's not be pessimistic," Lien said. "We can last a week if we don't move or do any drilling. But I'm positive we'll be able to replace the missing tracks and get back to Cross Station for additional supplies. After everything we've been through together, we're not going to let ourselves be stopped by a few wolves, are we?"

"It's not the wolves, but whatever it is that's behind them," said Farrell. "We haven't solved that mystery yet. You don't think that the wolves took away the rails, do you? Don't you remember what you saw the first day?"

"No, what did I see?" said Lien, sincerely.

"A Redfur. Suppose they're behind it..."

"How could you imagine they'd be able to do something like this? They have a deep aversion to everything technological. They'd never even dream of touching a rail. Besides, by now, most of them have learned that they're electrified and dangerous."

"Why do you insist on thinking that they're nothing but primitives? They've been around for a more than a hundred years. They've had time to evolve and learn. I think you're making a mistake."

"Let's not lose sight of what we need to do. Our first concern has to be to reestablish the line."

"Yeah. Our lifeline's been broken."

Lien felt all the helplessness expressed by that remark. He knew the feeling well; the deep anxiety that being separated from the Company could create. The Company was like a mother in whose bosom one felt safe and secure. On this ice-covered world, only the rails kept society together, and enabled mankind to survive. They carried power, and therefore heat; even those who didn't travel needed heat to survive. The most isolated farmers knew they only needed to link up to the Company's network to receive heat. There were very few Outsiders who chose to live independently of the Company, and even Lien had difficulty imagining how they could do it.

"Don't worry," Lien reassured his men. "We've been in worse situations before, and we'll get out of this one too."

A few timid smiles answered him, and the crew began to move around.

"First, we have to keep the wolves away. I'd estimate that to replace the line, we'll need at least half a day."

He turned towards Yann.

"We'll use your explosives, and the flame-throwers. Everything we have. We can also protect ourselves behind a barrier of burning liquid coal.

"It'll freeze before we can get it lit."

"Not if we keep it at the right temperature. I know it's dangerous, but if we keep it under high pressure, it won't be able to freeze. Wolves are afraid of fire. It's our best weapon."

Then, Lien asked the cook to get lunch ready.

"Make something solid," he said, trying to sound cheerful. "We'll need all our strength for the work ahead. We can iron out the details while we eat."

At first, it wasn't easy. The team ate in silence, almost reluctantly. Lien found it difficult to concentrate on the task at hand. Farrell, who had been behaving in a bizarre fashion since the start, seemed to be in better spirits and tried to help him.

"If we ride in the steam engine, and leave the rest of the train here, we'll only need light. That way, we'll gain some time."

The cook served wine with the food. Lien made sure everyone's glass was kept full, hoping that it would make the men feel more relaxed.

"Why don't we radio now?" Yann said, not wanting to let his idea go. "At least we could alert Security at Cross Station."

"I guess it wouldn't hurt," Lien said. "We'll call them to let them know what's happening out here, and tell them that we'll post regular reports."

"Shh," Lamont said suddenly. "Listen."

In spite of the car's insulation, from outside they could hear the howling of the wolves.

CHAPTER FIVE

Lien's radio call was answered by someone named Todd, a Security Sergeant at Cross Station. He listened attentively to Lien's story before answering.

"So, what is it you want exactly? A rescue team?"

"Not yet. We're going to try to get out of this by ourselves. But if we can't, we want to know that we can count on your help."

"Try not to," Todd replied. "We've been on alert since yesterday and we may not be able to get over there in time."

"On alert?" Lien said, surprised. "What's going on?"

"I can't tell you. Security. By the way, has any equipment been stolen?"

"Yes. Like I told you, the mobile switching system disappeared. I'd guess it was worth.."

"Forget the money. It's the strategic value that counts. You're going to be in big trouble when you get back."

"Strategic value? But we're thousands of miles away from the Front. How could..."

"You better get in here immediately to make a report, otherwise you're going to be in big trouble."

"What do you think we've been trying to do all this time?"

"Okay, but don't take advantage of the situation. We want you here tomorrow afternoon. Over and out."

The communication was cut off, and Lien turned to his companions.

"It sounds like we're just about being accused of sabotage," Farrell said indignantly

"I wonder why they're on alert," Lamont said. "And why he cared about the switch being stolen..."

When night fell they were still hard at work. Lien estimated that the new connection was almost finished, and that, at sunrise, they would be able to make it back to the main line. Throughout the night, the wolves' incessant howling grated on everybody's nerves.

Around three in the morning, Lien got out of bed and went to the dining room. He sat there alone and made himself a cup of tea.

Suddenly, Yann burst into the room.

"What's wrong?" Lien said, jumping to his feet.

"Look at this!"

The man unrolled a sheet of paper that he had just torn off the seismograph.

"We've just recorded it. It's showing activity on the other line, but it's not an earthquake. It's a train, a convoy over a mile long!"

"On this old deserted line? It's not even electrified!"

"Yeah. It must have been some kind of special convoy. That has to be the reason someone was trying to keep us away. They didn't want us to be in the way, or find out about it."

Lien tried to sort out his thoughts. Ever since the wolves had first appeared, they had all bombarded him with disturbing ideas, and evidence of strange possibilities. He no longer knew what to do.

"Listen, calm down and have a cup of tea. That line's been practically abandoned for years. It doesn't even go anywhere. Look it up in the Guide if you don't believe me. No farms, nothing. The Bia Sector is off-limits to almost everyone because of the problems with the ice. There are massive cliffs, and bottomless pits.

The line's barely able to carry a train like ours, four, maybe five cars. A mile-long convoy would have between thirty and forty cars; the rails just couldn't take it. The ties aren't even firmly anchored in the ice anymore and the whole thing would collapse. Even if it didn't, further on, the line is buried under mountains of ice, you hear me, mountains!"

"I know what I see," Yann said stubbornly. "My instruments don't lie. They recorded a seismic-like phenomenon on the line; the only thing that could account for it is a convoy. With the wolves and the air conditioning, we just couldn't hear it, that's all."

"But they would have had to have a steam engine."

"So?"

"No steam engine in existence could pull thirty or more cars," Lien said.

Their vehement argument had attracted the rest of the team. First Farrell and Lamont entered the dining room, the others followed. Everyone watched, confused.

"That's not true," replied Yann. "The big engines that pull the mobile palaces of the Company's big cheeses are all steam-powered. And what about F Station? How many engines did they use to drag that?"

"But they were electric engines."

"How do we know?"

Suddenly, Farrel raised his hands. The wolves' howling had stopped. On the table, Lien's cup was vibrating gently. He looked at it for a few seconds, then rushed to the airlock. Without taking the time to put on his isothermal suit, he opened the outside door. His doubts evaporated immediately. In the distance, he could hear the throbbing of the powerful engines, the creaking of the rails, the rattling and clanking of the wheels, the vibration of the ground. There was another huge train passing, and not very far away. Then, he passed out.

Someone pulled him out of the lock, closed the door and took him back to the dining room. In the space of less than a dozen seconds, because of the exposure to the outside temperature, his face had turned purple. They had to rub him with alcohol, and even give him an injection to stimulate the blood circulation on the right side of his face, which had begun to freeze.

When he came to, he was lying in his bed, wrapped in an electric blanket. Farrell was at his side, smiling.

"That was pretty stupid. You ought to know better."

"It was another convoy, wasn't it? But how could it have been? That line's been deserted for years."

"I know, but the seismograph confirmed it. It was almost one and a half miles long, in fact."

"That's impossible."

"Obviously not."

Lien sat up.

"Call Sergeant Todd. Tell him what we heard and ask for instructions."

"Okay. Do you need anything?"

Lien passed his hand over his face, and felt a soft tingling on it.

"No, I'll be okay. We've got to report this to Security. Two convoys travelling on an abandoned line are too big for us. Unless we were all hallucinating."

"Seismographs don't hallucinate."

"You're right, they don't," Lien said, pensively.

When Farrell returned, Lien was already up and walking around. He was surprised to see his assistant back so soon.

"The radio isn't working, but the equipment checks out. It's like trying to broadcast from inside a Faraday cage."

"Come on, that's impossible. We'd have to be inside a huge electro-magnetic field for..."

"Come and try it yourself then."

Lien did, and immediately saw that Farrell had been right. The signals didn't go through. His friend looked at him with fear in his eyes.

"What if it was the Siberians? What if they've broken through the Front? Or what if it's some kind of fifth column? Maybe they found a way though our lines so that they can strike at us from the back, with commandos or something."

"That's ridiculous."

The rest of the men had gathered around the seismograph, where Yann was explaining that he had fine tuned the machine since the passage of the two trains, so that now he would know if another train was coming at least ten minutes in advance.

"Are you sure about the length of those convoys? I still can't quite believe it. Trains that long on this antiquated line are just incredible."

"We live in an incredible world," Farrell said, rather pointlessly.

Yann confirmed the trains' length. Since his earlier outburst, he had completely calmed down, and now behaved with perfect, scientific detachment.

"I'd say they were each 1.4 miles to be accurate; between fifty and sixty cars."

"But only a regularly maintained line could carry that kind of traffic," Lien said.

Suddenly he felt the need to sit down. His bloodstream was probably still carrying some frozen tissue, and he risked a stroke just by walking around and getting too excited.

"Our duty..." he began.

It was ridiculous, of course, and he knew it almost as soon as he had said it. Even though the Company made survival possible for everyone in this merciless ice age, none of his men felt particularly loyal or devoted to it.

"We should warn Security," he finished lamely.

"What I find odd," Yann said, "is that the convoys were going towards the south, not the north."

Lien, his eyes closed, thought about Yann's remark. If he was right, Farrell's hypothesis that the Company was being secretly invaded no longer held true. Heading towards the south, the line led nowhere. It was a total mystery.

"Okay," he said finally. "In any event, it's an anomaly and should be reported."

He grabbed a copy of the Guide.

"According to the Official Railway Guide, line S 68 has two Xs next to it. That means it's been officially closed, even though it wasn't thought worthwhile to dismantle it. It looks like there used to be a small privately operated coal mine at the other end, but that looks like it was closed five years ago. It was dug inside a mountain whose top was well above ice level. Apparently it was running in the red, and the Company refused to subsidize the cost of running the line, so they just closed down the mine and moved away."

That was the end of the discussion. There weren't any other incidents during the night, and at last they were able to get a couple of hours of sound sleep.

As dawn approached, they got up and drove the loco-car to the point where the rails had been removed.

They went outside in their isothermal suits to confront the mob of hungry wolves. As soon as they began using the flame-throwers, the beasts backed away, this enabled them to install more permanent fire barriers on either side of the rails. Then, they quickly reassembled the remainder of the line with the help of a small crane mounted on the loco-car. The reinstallation of a switch required more time and finesse, but the fire kept the wolves at bay, in spite of their quite visible hunger.

"I'll try the radio again," said Farrell.

Five minutes later, he returned, this time wearing a smile on his face.

"It's working. I got our friend Sergeant Todd. He sounded like he didn't believe me, and ordered us back to Cross Station immediately."

"We're working on it, we're working on it," Lien grumbled, watching as the final adjustments were made to the switching apparatus.

Then, at noon, the loco-car was finally able to cross back onto line S 68 XX. There, they immediately noticed traces of the previous night's convoys. The line had been badly damaged, but was still useable. Once again Lien found himself pondering the mystery of two one-and-a-half mile long trains, travelling southward on an abandoned line. They moved cautiously at first, but the rails held up.

It wasn't until they left S 68 and returned to Secondary Line 34 that Lien felt better, however. The first sign of civilization, an impoverished and isolated farm-train, was greeted by the team with an ovation.

"I took the seismograph tapes, in case they don't believe us," said Yann. Then, he added, "I wonder if we'll ever find out what was going on..."

"I don't know," Lien said. "Have you ever heard anything about the Oblique Road?"

"The same as everyone else, I guess. Do you think we found it by accident?"

Lien shrugged. Ever since his team had been asked to survey Bia Sector, strange events had occurred. The daughter of the Seventeenth District's Governor had invited him to a party, taken him to meet some outsiders, made love to him and even gotten him a steam-powered engine. He couldn't quite bring himself to believe that his charm was the only thing that had motivated the mysterious Floa.

"We'll be at Cross Station in an hour," Lamont informed them, while watching the controls.

Although 34 was only a Secondary line, they were joined by a dozen other sets of tracks as they got closer to the Station.

"Hey!" Lamont called out, "we're being overridden."

Lien wasn't overly worried; he thought that Security wanted to question them before they had a chance to tell anyone else their story.

"We're not even going to Cross Station," Lamont remarked. "We're being sent somewhere else."

"When I spoke to him on the radio, Sergeant Todd said they were on alert. Maybe something happened at Cross Station?"

"A livestock trading town?" Yann said, looking unconvinced. "What could happen there? A fight between breeders and traders over the cost of reindeer meat? No, it has to be something else."

They were now heading away from Cross Station, towards the east. Somebody joked that they were being sent to the Front, but nobody laughed.

Lamont was carefully combing the Guide for clues.

"We're not travelling on any line I can find. I can't even get an idea of where we are or where we're going..."

It was a small line, with only two tracks. They saw no other trains from either direction, not even a patrol car or maintenance engine. Suddenly, the line sloped downward thirty degrees, and took them between two steep ice cliffs.

"Hey, it's getting tricky."

"Reverse steam."

"I already did that."

"We should have stopped a long time ago."

"We still can."

"No, not on this kind of line, it's probably a violation." Lien said. "We need to find a siding."

He, too, began feverishly looking through the Guide, but without success. Suddenly, it was pitch-black, and Lamont switched on the lights.

"An ice tunnel!"

Ice tunnels were rare but not unheard of, and they were always dangerous. This tunnel, however, was not typical.

"No, look, it's a tunnel actually dug into the rock," Yann said. "We're travelling underground, and at a constant speed."

Lien looked at his watch; it was now two hours since they had been deflected from Cross Station. If it had been a routine matter, Station Security would have been able to handle it. This bizarre voyage indicated that they were involved in something that was serious enough to cause the Company to override their yellow box, sending them to a more confidential investigation center. Maybe even to a military outpost.

Finally the engine slowed and came to a stop next to a small platform on a siding that ended at the tunnel's rocky wall.

"Doesn't look like anyone's here."

"Don't worry. Somebody will show up."

Indeed, they suddenly saw the powerful lights of a much larger train. A minute later, one of the Company's dreadnoughts came to a standstill next to them. A mobile airlock was put in place to connect the two trains, and a half dozen armed guards burst into the room.

"Hands up, all of you!" shouted a fierce-looking officer.

"I'm Glaciologist Lien Rag. I have a report to..."

The officer lifted his fist, and smashed Lien in the face. His teammates tried to defend him, but the threat of the armed guards forced them to reconsider. Lien had fallen to the floor, where he lay, wiping blood off his mouth.

"Take them across!"

"You can't! I'm responsible for this train!" Lien managed to say, in spite of his swollen mouth.

No one paid any attention to him and, soon afterwards, they were all locked up in a cell aboard the dreadnought. The train began to move with so much power that they lost their footing, the momentum pushing them up against the opposite wall.

"This looks pretty bad," Lien told them, "I think this time we're in real trouble."

"But we haven't committed any crime!"

Lien shrugged.

"We all know we haven't, but what counts is what Security thinks. They wouldn't have acted like this if they didn't think we were guilty of something."

The dreadnought travelled steadily for half-an-hour. Since there were no windows in their cell, Lien and his men had no idea whether they were moving underground or on the surface. Even Yann, who usually had an unerring sense of direction, couldn't figure out where they were going.

"We're slowing down."

The dreadnought must have hooked up to a larger train, because they felt, and heard, the characteristic shock. A few minutes later, the officer who had boarded their loco-car entered their cell and made them put their hands on their heads.

"Follow me!" he ordered.

They crossed an expandable airlock and then walked down a long corridor until they reached an antechamber. There were still no windows to enable them to see where they were. Some plastic chairs were lined up against the wall, and they were ordered to sit in these. The wait began.

Suddenly an invisible voice called out, "Glaciologist Lien Rag."

Two guards took Lien and pushed him through a door that, up until then, had been invisible. He found himself in a small office where everything seemed to be made of metal, and assumed they were now inside a military train.

A fat man sitting behind an almost totally bare desk looked at him severely. From the markings on his sleeve, Lien could see he held the rank of Major.

"Come closer."

He obeyed. The Major pushed a button on his desk and a hologram appeared behind him.

"Do you know this man?"

Lien studied the picture. It was obviously a uniformed Security officer.

"I never met him before in my life, but from his uniform I can tell he's a Sergeant."

"You're lying. It's Sergeant Todd.'

"I never met him, but it's true we talked to him on the radio. We reported some difficulties we ran into on S 68. We heard two unreported convoys passing by last night, even though the line is classified XX and..."

"Shut up. Todd is being charged with selling fuel vouchers on the black market, and you used your communication as a coded system to let him know you were ready to sell him your vouchers."

Lien was flabbergasted by the absurdity of the accusation.

"That's preposterous! I never even met Sergeant Todd!"

"They gave you fuel vouchers at Grand Star Station. What did you do with them?"

"I don't have them on me, if that's what you mean. But they're in my train. We had to leave quickly and..."

"You're lying again," the Major said. "You sold them. You were approached by a notorious black marketer in Cross Station."

A new hologram appeared, showing the face of the man who had, indeed, offered to buy the vouchers.

"Well, that's true but..."

"You're confessing."

"I don't have anything to confess, I turned him down. I'm against the black market."

The Major shook his head.

"You're lying. We have the proof. You sold four vouchers for a thousand dollars. What did you do with the money?"

"That's not true! I never sold anything! We've had some strange things happen to us in the last week, but they had nothing to do with the black market. We heard two trains go by on a line that was supposed to be closed and..."

"Two trains, you say. Really. How long?" the Major said with a condescending look in his eyes.

"Over a mile and a half long each. Yann, one of my assistants, can prove it. He has seismographic readouts."

The Major laughed so brazenly that Lien felt like jumping on the desk, strangling him and pounding his face with his fists. He was surprised by this unexpected urge; how could he experience such strong, violent feelings?

"A train over a mile and a half long on a XX line... That's absurd!"

The Major stopped laughing and looked at Lien, his eyes filled with pity and contempt.

"Your story is absurd. Nobody will believe you."

"What about the tapes?"

"Faked, obviously."

"I swear that..."

"You're mad, Lien Rag, completely mad."

"I guarantee you that we can back up our story of everything that happened in the Bia Sector with solid, scientific evidence."

"Solid, scientific evidence! You, fool!"

"Why are you insulting me?" Lien shouted back.

The Major appeared somewhat taken aback by Lien's outburst, but recovered quickly.

"I'm formally charging you with illegally selling Company property on the black market."

CHAPTER SIX

Lien was locked up in a perfectly insulated padded cell. Because all the train's noises and vibrations were, therefore, silenced, he was kept in total ignorance as to the details of his imprisonment. He remained in this complete isolation for two days, receiving his food and water through a slot in the door, where, because of a double shutter system, he could not even see the face of the person delivering it to him.

Although they had taken away his watch, he was able to keep a rough track of the time. He thought for a moment about Floa Sadon, who had a timepiece powered by her nervous system grafted onto her arm.

In the middle of the second day they came for him and forced him into a straight jacket, which worried him considerably. Were they really going to treat him as if he were mad, and lock him away in a psychiatric train? These moved endlessly throughout the Company without ever stopping, and the same was true of prisons for common criminals. Only concentration camps for political prisoners were located for long periods of time in faraway Districts, usually near the Arctic Circle.

When he was led back into the Major's office, he saw that he wasn't alone. There was another prisoner there, and from the hologram he had seen earlier, he recognized Sergeant Todd. The Major was there too. This time, he was wearing a name tag identifying him as "Vicra."

"Do you still deny that you were involved in black marketeering with this man, Glaciologist Lien Rag?"

"I do. You'll find all the vouchers I was given in my desk back at my train in the Bia Sector."

"We searched it and found nothing. Sergeant Todd confessed too. He told us you sold him four vouchers for a thousand dollars. The intermediary was a long-haired outsider named Szabo. So far, we haven't been able to catch him, but Todd here has admitted that Szabo was working for him."

"I don't believe what's happening! This is all some kind of nightmare!" Lien shouted. "I never met Sergeant Todd, I only spoke to him on the radio, and never about the black market. This is nothing but a fabrication -- a frame-up! I'll appeal!"

"I'd advise you to watch what you say," Major Vicra said. "You were properly notified that any unauthorized sale of fuel vouchers is a wartime offense. I'm the only judge of your case, and I'm also the only one who will determine what your sentence will be."

"Everything is a wartime offense! The war never ends!"

"Those are dangerous political statements, prisoner Rag. And false too. We've had three truces in the last ten years."

"Then no one told me about them," Lien replied sarcastically. But he realized he was playing into the Major's hands by arguing with him. He had to keep denying everything, and request that a proper investigation be made of the mysterious events that had taken place on Line S 68 XX.

"I deny Sergeant Todd's testimony," he finally said with quiet strength. "He belongs to Security and could have been subject to all kinds of pressure. I also ask that my companions be heard in testimony on my behalf, and in particular, Glaciologist Farrell, and technicians Yann Charm and Lamont Vernier. The events that took place on Line S 68 XX are far more important than this stupid accusation of black marketeering."

"I'm the one who will decide if an accusation is, as you say, stupid or not. As for your companions, they've already signed a deposition stating that there was only one train on Line S 68 XX -- yours! It is patently absurd to pretend that any convoys could travel on a XX line. Your companions have also added that you were exhibiting signs of increased -- and suspect -- nervousness prior to the so-called incidents."

"What about the seismic tapes?"

"Our experts examined them. What they show was caused by a completely normal contraction of the ice. As you know, the Bia Sector is littered with crevices and underground chasms, which cause constant dilatations and contractions. As a Class-2 Glaciologist you're certainly not going to deny that this is true?"

Lien remained silent. Such contractions could indeed occur, but what they had heard and recorded were not a natural phenomenon but the evidence of a passing train.

"We found traces of the train on the line itself," he said. "They conform exactly to what I described."

"Really?" the Major said, his voice dripping with irony, while Sergeant Todd laughed obsequiously. "None of your men reported seeing such traces. In any event, a load of thousands of tons couldn't possibly travel on a XX line. Besides, as you well know, that line is no longer electrified. Only steam-powered engines of the first magnitude could pull a train of the size you described, and they're all carefully registered and accounted for."

Until now, Lien had thought they were only trying to force him to deny having seen or heard unreported convoys on the abandoned line, in order not to panic people with a rumor that there were trains circulating about which the Company knew nothing. He had also wondered if they might not have accidentally discovered that mysterious Oblique Road, which was a seriously frowned upon myth. But suddenly, he began to understand that what had really happened on Line S 68 XX must have been something much more serious, something with darker implications for Security.

He realized he had to rein in his impetuosity, and behave in a more careful and cunning fashion, or else they would simply get rid of him.

"I thought that some illegal faction had taken possession of a couple of trains," he said. "I was only trying to do my duty by reporting it."

"You made up this whole story simply to cover up your trafficking," the Major replied. "If Sergeant Todd here hadn't come forward, you might have gotten away with it. But now we have you, and unless you confess, you'll be sentenced to five years of hard labor."

Lien still didn't understand why the Company had let him go into the Bia Sector if it really was an area that was considered top secret by Security. It would have been easier to get him and his men out of the way by giving them a last minute change in orders and sending them someplace else.

Suddenly, Floa's role in all this took on a more ominous meaning. Maybe she hadn't acted unselfishly at all by getting him a steam engine. There was also that remark Governor Sadon himself had made at the party. The man had seemed almost impatient for him to visit the Bia Sector to study the increase in the thickness of the ice. He had even dangled the promise of a promotion to Class-1. But suppose there had been another, more mysterious reason. If that were so, Security, taken by surprise, had had to concoct a last minute scheme to eliminate him and his team.

"You're excused, Sergeant Todd. Your cooperative attitude will count for much in my report. There will be a demerit appended to your file, but you won't be demoted."

"Thank you, Sir. I'm eternally grateful."

It occurred to Lien that he wasn't even sure that the man really was Sergeant Todd. It could have been anyone and, having played his part, he was now exiting the scene.

He was alone with the Major, and was waiting for him to pass sentence when, suddenly, the officer pulled out another file which he read for a couple of minutes. Then he raised his eyes and looked at Lien craftily.

"I see here that you've intrigued for a long time to get a steam engine. Your first request is two years old, and you kept filing one after the other. Eventually, you had no scruples about abusing the good faith of Company dignitaries to reach your miserable ends."

"But it's not true!" Lien said, forgetting his own resolution to be more careful. "I know that the daughter of the Seventeenth District's Governor interceded on my behalf, but I didn't ask her to do it."

The feeling that Vicra was playing a cat and mouse game came over him. He had once seen these almost extinct animals in a zoo and, at the time, had felt sorry that he couldn't own one himself. At the beginning of the new ice age, most of the cats had died from the cold, or had fallen prey to wilder, fiercer species. This, in part, accounted for the fact that the rats now thrived.

"You didn't ask, you say. Are you telling me that Floa Sadon, daughter of his Excellency, the Governor of the Seventeenth District, used her influence on your behalf to get you an LB 117 steam engine and fuel vouchers?"

Lien backtracked as fast as he could.

"Frankly, I don't know. I'd filed an application and Lieutenant Skoll told me I'd have to wait at least a week. Then, the next day he called me in to tell me my request had been granted."

"But did you know that you owed it to Floa Sadon?"

"Lieutenant Skoll did say that the Governor himself had interceded on my behalf. And the night before, I had been invited to a party at the Governor's palace where he, himself, told me he wanted a prompt study of the ice situation in the Bia Sector."

"The Governor said this?"

"That's what I understood, yes," Lien said, liking the expression on Vicra's face less and less.

"Had you known his daughter for a long time before this?"

"No. In fact, I only met her that very same night."

"That very same night... I know that people are more promiscuous today, but don't you think that was a bit fast to become her lover?"

Lien decided not to answer that one. The Major chuckled and looked at another sheet.

"I see here that you attended an Outsiders party about one hundred twenty miles from Grand Star Station. One of the people at the meeting was a young woman named Ariel, who's been convicted of bestiality."

"Bestiality?"

"She's had regular sexual intercourse with Redfurs. That's an offense that carries a penalty of ten years imprisonment, followed by psychiatric rehabilitation."

"Redfurs aren't animals, you know."

He could have bitten his tongue for that last, stupid remark. Vicra leaned back in his chair and smiled widely. His teeth were too perfect to be true. They had to be false.

"Really. So you don't think they're animals?"

"No, I don't."

"So, you support this girl's depraved behavior; you get a kick out of picturing her being penetrated by those monsters' enormous organs?"

Instinctively, Lien experienced a brief but powerful feeling of disgust, in spite of what his mind was telling him. He couldn't help but scowl for a brief instant. Later, he would regret this involuntary gesture, which had shown the despicable Major that he, too, somewhere deep inside himself, felt the same way about the Ice People. But at the time, it seemed to please the officer, who changed the subject.

"Floa Sadon has many suspicious people in her entourage."

"I had no idea where she was taking me when we left the Governor's party."

As he said it, he felt like a coward, shifting the blame to Floa. But, once again, the Major seemed to be pleased by this display of baser instincts, and actually smiled at him.

"I'll grant you that point. However, the fact remains that you didn't report her, or what happened that night, to Security, and primarily because you were hoping to use her to get you a steam engine."

"Not at all. I'll be frank with you. She's a damned attractive girl, and the only thing in my mind at the time was to go to bed with her."

"So, you did."

"It's really none of your business."

The Major flashed a salacious smile.

"Is she frigid like they say?"

This time, Lien kept quiet. He had learned his lesson with the question about the Redfurs, and didn't want to betray Floa any further. She had seemed to enjoy their lovemaking, but in the end, he wasn't certain that she hadn't faked it.

"Does she have sexual intercourse with the Redfurs too? It's quite a fashionable perversion these days, one that's hard to fight. I've even heard that some of the high society ladies keep their own, private Redfurs in cages as studs, to satisfy their wicked passions."

Suddenly, he realized that he was almost fantasizing aloud, and his attitude changed radically; his face grew stern and his tone brutal.

"You saw how Sergeant Todd got out of trouble? He did his duty by informing on you. You can do the same, and inform on others. There are some who believe this Company has had enough of being exploited by a class of idle parasites who think only of their own pleasure. It's time we got rid of them, even if they occupy important positions or belong to respectable families."

Lien listened carefully, his heart thumping in his chest. Was Major Vicra offering him a way out of his predicament, if he was willing to inform on Floa?

"Are you sure that Floa Sadon didn't manifest any perverted, unnatural desire for the Redfurs?"

"I don't know."

"There was an Ice Man at the meeting you attended. Do you know why these people always invite them; especially the males? It's because they're excited by the sight of their genitals. The Redfurs are animals, formidably endowed by nature, but animals nevertheless. I'm certain that Floa Sadon copulated with them."

Lien felt a wave of disgust wash over him. The Ice People weren't animals. And after all, Floa was perfectly free to make love with whomever she pleased. Why should the Company care? As far as he was concerned, whether she liked getting her kicks with Redfurs, women or even wolves, that was her business and hers only, not the Company's. He decided not to give in to the Major's pressure.

"If we had an eyewitness testimony," the Major continued, "we could put a stop to her scandalous behavior. I'm sure Security would be extremely grateful to you, Glaciologist Rag, think about it..."

"You're despicable," Lien said quietly.

CHAPTER SEVEN

Even when they had tortured him the most mercilessly, Lien never lost consciousness, something that he
much regretted. With an unbearable feeling of horror, he
had remained aware during the painful ministrations carried out on him by the Security officers. Major Vicra had
not taken kindly to being called despicable, but he was
even angrier about Lien's refusal to inform on Floa Sadon. Lien had no idea why the Major was so intent on
convicting the Governor's daughter of bestiality or cor-
ruption. However, he had used his refusal to testify as a
last refuge, and not without a certain degree of calcula-
tion. He was completely aware that if anyone had the
power to intercede and rescue him from Security, it was
the Governor. He may not have felt chivalrous enough to
happily withstand the torments inflicted upon him for the
sake of the beautiful Floa, but he realized that she could
well be his last chance, and was therefore forced to take
her side.

For a few seconds, they had exposed his naked
body to the outside temperatures. He had felt his limbs
grow numb from the sub-zero cold, and his life begin to
ebb away. Then, they had subjected him to brutally high
temperatures. They had also given him electric shocks
that, for forty-eight hours, came intermittently at all
times of day and night. Anticipating the next shock,
which could come a second or hours from the one before, had been excruciatingly nerve-wracking. Yet, he
had not given up.

His gambit paid off, however, because suddenly,
with an air of panic, they rushed him to an infirmary.
They took good care of him, showing absolutely no ma-

lice, and his hopes were beginning to rise when they ordered him to dress, then took him to a small penitentiary train that was leaving for the north.

He found himself in a cell in the company of two other prisoners who appeared to be common criminals. One had killed his children, and the other was a black marketeer.

The train stopped for two days on a siding, before continuing on its journey to an extremely small station of little importance called Pipeline Station, probably because either a liquid coal or oil pipeline ran through it.

Through the small window of their cell, where the temperature was kept at a minimum, Lien could see an antiquated dome. It really was a rat hole, and for the first time, he began to lose hope. He had prayed that, sooner or later, Floa Sadon would hear about his arrest, and that she would intervene on his behalf. But obviously, that had not happened. Neither he, nor his name, must have meant much to whatever the Governor or his daughter was plotting. Chances were strong that he would spend the rest of his life in a penitentiary or, worse, an arctic concentration camp.

Just before noon, a warden and two guards appeared to open the gate and take the prisoners out; no one dared to refuse. He hadn't yet been told with what kind of crime he had been charged, nor to what sentence he had been condemned. He still hoped to force the penitentiary administration into telling him the truth. He had even thought of using passive resistance and hunger strikes.

"Where are you taking me?"

"You're being transferred to another train."

However, they gave him some poorly cut civilian clothes before, accompanied by a single guard, he was allowed onto the platform without any chains or other surveillance. In a state of uncertainty, he was taken to another, smaller, train, almost certainly a local omnibus. It was an older machine dragging four miserable-looking cars with rundown heating units and without adequate insulation. He was sure it would be freezing inside once it left the Station's airlock. The guard told Lien to sit between a fat woman who was nursing a baby and a pimply teenager. For a minute, he felt as if he had been transported into one of those ancient films he had seen long ago, where country people were caricatured in much this same way.

"Where are we going?" he asked out loud.

But no one answered him. They had seen him enter escorted by the guard and they distrusted him. Even the woman who was nursing hid her breast, as if the sight of the blue-veined organ would inspire him with ideas of rape.

Fifteen minutes later, the omnibus started slowly and irregularly. As he had expected, the temperature drastically dropped to forty degrees as soon as it left the Station. Everyone wrapped themselves in heavy blankets, while he alone remained shivering in his light clothes.

The train stopped at every farm, so the cars emptied progressively. Soon, the only other person left in his car was the teenager. He smiled shyly.

"We're going to River Station."

Lien reacted in amazement.

"The capital of the Seventeenth District?" he said, not believing his own luck.

"Yes, of course. I'm a student there, but I've just been drafted."

Taking notice of Lien's plight, the student opened his luggage and handed him a blanket.

"Has the Governor's palace gotten back?" the Glaciologist asked after he had wrapped himself up comfortably.

"I don't know. I just spent two weeks with my folks. When I was there last, it hadn't."

Lien suddenly realized that less than two weeks had gone by since he had left Grand Star Station.

"We'll be there in a couple of hours. Do you want something to eat? My mother gave me some chicken."

Normally, Lien hated the bland taste of chicken, but this time, he found the meat had a savor it had never had before. The boy, pleased to have someone to talk to, began to describe his studies. He was preparing to become a doctor.

"I have a Security scholarship. I'll be a military doctor."

Lien had bitter thoughts for the military doctors who had contributed to his torture. In Security, a doctor's work wasn't limited to just caring for the sick.

"Wouldn't you rather be a civilian doctor?"

"Well, yes, but you see, my folks didn't have enough money to pay for my studies, so a scholarship was the only answer."

Finally, the train arrived at River Station. There, the Glaciologist was greeted by an impressive loco-car and one of the Governor's servants, who looked at him disdainfully because of his clothes, and seemed surprised he was travelling without luggage.

"Are you taking me to the palace?"

"No, not exactly."

Without being as big as Grand Star Station, River Station was, nevertheless, a major city. Hundreds of rail lines intersected there, and it was a beehive of activity. Because it was a district capital, there were numerous administration trains, some of which had probably never left the dome. Lien wondered how the civil servants could stand to spend their entire lives in such a place. Obviously, there were cabarets, restaurants and other fun places, but the number of such distractions must have been limited. And, in such a provincial city, everyone probably quickly got to know everyone else.

The loco-car stopped in front of a powerful-looking train which occupied at least four lines. Lien had already noticed that the temperature in River Station was even higher than that of Grand Star Station. Then he remembered that several years ago there had been major geothermic drilling done in the area; he even remembered seeing the reports in the professional journals.

A young woman greeted him respectfully and took him to a spacious bedroom, with a luxurious bathroom located on a mezzanine.

"The Doctor will be with you in a few minutes."

"The Doctor?"

"Miss Sadon's instructions."

He remained alone, playing with the various taps and smelling the colored bars of soap, until he heard a knock on the door. When he opened it, a tall man with bright blue eyes and a nonchalant attitude was standing there.

"I'm supposed to examine you. Get undressed and lie down on the bed."

Lien sighed, but did as he was asked.

"You could use a shower," the Doctor said, without sounding reproachful.

"I was in prison. I spent four days in Security's hands."

"I couldn't care less. I'm just here to see if you're okay. I don't want any trouble with Security. Floa is sometimes a little too reckless for my taste."

Lien was rapidly growing annoyed with the man's uncaring attitude.

"You mean, you don't care that I've been tortured."

"Everyone with a gripe against Security complains about torture."

That was more than Lien could take. He got up and opened the door.

"Get out!~" he shouted.

"Hey, don't get upset... I didn't know it meant so much to you."

"Get out right now!"

"No, thank you, I want to keep my job. If I upset you, I apologize. What are these burn marks on your testicles?"

Lien felt like strangling him.

"What do you think? Have you ever heard of electric shock torture?"

"I see. Hmm... It doesn't look too serious. But it can't have been a hell of a lot of fun for you."

"Are you employed by the Governor?"

"In a way. I work for the local second class Company hospital. The first class hospital was sent to the Front for six months. I don't really care, since I was discharged last year. I see from your right leg that you've been to the Front too. Okay. I'll write in my report that you really were mistreated by Security."

"You don't seem too hot about it."

The Doctor put his instruments back in his bag, thought for a minute then turned.

"No, I'm not too hot about getting caught up in some kind of internecine political fight between the various factions vying for power. I don't own any Company shares. Do you?"

Lien shook his head. He remembered that Floa was one of the Trans-European's major stockholders. But why had the Doctor brought up this point in the discussion?

"New shares used to be routinely issued and given as a reward to people deemed worthy; the Company had decided to increase the number of stockholders. But some political factions have recently pointed out the danger of spreading the Company's capital too thin. It's like it was in the democracy of the pre-Ice Age days, power always remains the privilege of a few individuals or groups. The same with stock."

"I don't understand."

The Doctor looked at him, his eyes full of contemptuous pity.

"So you don't know why you've been tortured?"

"No. Why are you talking about stock? I don't own any either."

But the Doctor only grumbled under his breath and left. Thinking about what he had said, Lien went back to the bathroom and filled the tub. Once soaking in the hot water, he was filled with a feeling of utter well being and closed his eyes. His thoughts kept returning to the matter of Company politics.

"You don't look like you're in such bad shape," a woman's voice said suddenly.

He recognized her perfume as well as her voice. He opened his eyes and saw her, leaning against the door, the mocking smile on her lips betrayed by a more tender expression in the depths of her green eyes. She was wearing a floor-length coat of black wolf skin, which permitted only the tips of her black leather boots to emerge. Lien experienced the odd thought that even six months of his salary wouldn't be enough to keep this woman in the lifestyle she took for granted.

"I just read the Doctor's report. They don't seem to have damaged you too much."

"Otherwise you'd have stayed away?"

"Of course not. But they could have done much worse. Infect you with some kind of disease. Castrate you. Relatively speaking, you've been treated pretty gently."

Remembering the torture that he'd gone though, Lien was angered by Floa's almost clinical evaluation. Still completely naked, he stood up in the tub.

"As you can see, all my parts are still in place."

"Indeed. But I see some burns," she observed. Then she flashed a very perverse smile. "How was it to be tortured there. Does it really hurt? Is it true that sometimes, you experience so much pain that you actually have an orgasm?"

Disgusted, Lien wrapped himself in a towel and quickly walked past her, back into the bedroom.

"You shouldn't take it so hard," Floa said. "You should be grateful instead. Without my father and me, you'd be rotting away in one of their penitentiaries, without any hope of getting out."

"I know what I owe you," he replied rather curtly. "Keep reminding me."

Floa frowned, and Lien realized that she wasn't accustomed to seeing him bitter and hostile. She had known him as a secure and somewhat nonchalant glaciologist, and his transformation must have seemed very strange to her. He tried to appear more conciliatory.

"I'm sorry, but one of the reasons they grabbed me was precisely because of your intervention with Lieutenant Skoll to get me a steam engine. Also, they tried to get me to inform on you, to charge you with all sorts of crimes, and I wouldn't."

In spite of her make-up, Lien could see Floa suddenly become very pale.

"Major Vicra. It was Major Vicra, wasn't it?"

"Yes. Why are they after you?"

Suddenly, he began to understand the meaning of the Doctor's earlier remarks. The political context in which he had been arrested and tortured finally became clear to him.

"Forget all that," she said. "You're out of danger now. You'll be reintegrated into your job, and reassigned to the Glaciologist Corps of this district. That'll keep you safe."

"Under your father?"

"Indirectly, but you'll be free."

"Why did you all want me to go to the Bia Sector?"

"Now, come on that's not fair," she said, pouting like a small girl. "Instead of asking all these questions, we should be celebrating. I was so looking forward to us getting back together. Have you forgotten the night we spent together?"

"Did you ever make love to a Redfur like they said?"

"Are you crazy? Why are you insulting me?"

She had expressed the same feeling of innate disgust at the idea as he had, when Major Vicra had suggested it. It was the same racist reflex; something that came from deep within and couldn't lie.

"I'm not like that bitch, Ariel!"

"Security wanted me to testify that you were guilty of bestiality among other things," Lien said. "Why are they so intent on getting rid of you? What have you done to them?"

"Later," she said, getting closer to him. "Later."

"Does it have something to do with stock?"

Floa stopped and looked at him coldly.

"Sometimes you surprise me. You're less stupid than you look."

"You own quite a chunk of Company stock, don't you? I guess you attend board meetings, and cast a major vote."

She remained silent. Instead, she opened her coat. Beneath, she was completely naked, except for the leather boots, which wrapped her legs to mid-thigh.

She snuggled up to him and, with her long, delicate fingers started to gently remove his towel. She began caressing him.

"No permanent damage, I see," she purred.

He embraced her and kissed her violently, first on the mouth, then he knelt and began to kiss the rest of her magnificent body.

This time around, he was convinced that the rumors he had heard about her frigidity were false. He would never forget the sight of her, naked, except for her black leather boots and fur skin, first standing up, her back arched with sensuality then later, spread over the large bed, writhing in the throes of erotic pleasure.

When he woke up, night had fallen. At first, he thought she had gone, but she hadn't. She was curled up in the far corner of the bed, sleeping peacefully. In spite of her leather boots, she looked like a child.

CHAPTER EIGHT

When Lien and Floa awoke, they were both hungry. She suggested that they go to her club for a late dinner.

"It's only a half-hour from here. You'll see, it's a wonderful place."

"Another meeting place for outsiders?"

"The membership fee is five thousand dollars."

"Excuse me!" he replied.

He put on some expensive clothes that he found in the closet. Floa had picked them with her usual good taste. Then they went down to take her loco-car, which was waiting on a private platform. She still wore only her fur coat and boots, and Lien couldn't help but feel jealous of the looks other men gave her.

For a second he raised his eyes towards the dome and, through the ice, saw the ever-present shapes.

"You're looking at the Redfurs," she said. "Is it because of what Major Vicra said?"

"No. I can't help asking myself why they're here. Where do they come from? Where were they a hundred years ago?"

"You ask yourself too many questions to be happy."

They left the dome, the loco-car rushing through the misty polar night. There was a permanent fog caused by the cold, outside air seeping through deep crevices down into the hidden, warmer layers of ice.

Because it operated with a black box, Floa's loco-car was able to use the major network lines without even slowing down. As it passed by, signals flashed red, stopping dozens of other convoys. Finally, it left the network to take a double line heading straight west. In the distance, Lien saw a gleaming dome, which he thought might be a farm. But the rail line went directly towards it.

"That's the club," Floa said.

As they came out of the airlock, Lien thought he was dreaming, or watching one of those old movies where the colors were too bright and vivid. They stepped out of the loco-car directly onto a beach complete with palm trees, a vast expanse of white sand, and several straw bungalows where naked people were busy eating.

"It's hot in here," he remarked.

"Ninety degrees. Take off your clothes or you'll melt."

She took off her fur coat and walked towards a bungalow. Although everyone was equally naked, heads still turned when she passed. Floa was a stunning sight, with her long legs clad in their leather boots. Lien followed her advice and began to get undressed.

The bungalow was made up of two rooms and a bath. A servant dressed in a bright, flower-decorated kind of skirt, and wearing a flower in her hair, was already there, waiting to help them.

"Everything's done in the Tahitian style here," she explained. "Have you heard of Tahiti? It was an island in the Pacific. You must have seen it in a movie."

They were given coconuts filled with a vanilla-tasting drink.

"Rum," Floa said. "Should we go for a dip?"

"I can't believe it! It looks like we're on a beach... On some kind of ocean..."

"It's an optical illusion, done with holograms. The dome is actually less than fifteen hundred feet away, but it's enough. Amazing, isn't it?"

He looked up and saw a very convincing, faked blue sky.

"Another illusion. You can't see your friends the Redfurs here, but they're out there, cleaning the dome."

She ran towards the water, and he followed her. He had been in swimming pools before, but had never experienced anything so extraordinary.

"We can surf over there if you want to; they have wave-making machines."

After a while they went back to lie in the sand. She closed her eyes and offered her body to the warmth of the ambient atmosphere.

"What do you really know about this stock ownership business," she asked suddenly.

"Frankly, not much," he admitted.

"It's better that way," she said. "It's enough for you to know that Security is attempting to buy back any stock that's currently in the hands of small bearers. You know, those people who got one or two shares as a reward for twenty years of faithful service, things like that."

"Yeah. Like if you got a Medal of Honor at the Front, you used to get ten shares in the Company."

"Exactly. We stopped doing that, because the proliferation of small stockholders was a potential danger to us all."

"So the concern about spreading the Company's capital too far was just a lie," he said sarcastically.

"Yes. The real danger is that a person or a group could put pressure on those people to force them to sell their stock. What they should have done at the time was to create a special class of stock that couldn't be sold, at least for a while. But the inequality of status between the big holders and the small ones would have been too obvious."

Lien turned his head and admired Floa's regal profile.

"How much stock do you own anyway?"

"It's none of your business," she said calmly. "Security has discreetly been trying to acquire a lot of stock. If they succeed, the Company will turn into a military dictatorship."

"And it isn't already?"

"Oh, please! If it was, you wouldn't be here with me today. We keep Security in check."

"Why did you really send me to the Bia Sector?"

She sat up and encircled her knees with her arms.

"We'd had some disturbing information about something that was going to happen on that abandoned line... But we didn't specifically send you. My father thought an expedition to study the ice would be a perfect cover, and fate brought you to us at the right time. I wanted to meet you, to see what kind of man you were. I thought that if something strange or dangerous happened, you wouldn't lose control of yourself. And I was right."

"I almost died."

"So you see; I was right. What did happen out there?"

He told her about the wolves, and the stolen rails, and the mysterious passage of the two convoys. She shuddered.

"Are you sure?"

"Yes. But Major Vicra told me I was crazy."

"That's all so strange. That line is classified XX in the Guide. I even looked in the District's library and found information from twenty years ago. Even then it was thought to be unsafe, because of the movement of the ice. But the mine was only closed five years ago."

"At one point, I thought we had found the famous Oblique Road."

She smiled condescendingly. Lien sat up and looked around. A couple of hundred people were gathered on the beach; families, lovers, even old people.

"Are they all major shareholders?" he inquired.

"No. Just very rich people. You can be rich, even richer than me, and still not own any stock. There are industrialists here who are happy with the power they have in their own businesses and aren't at all interested in Company politics. But this whole place belongs to the Company."

"How many major stockholders are there then?"

"Maybe a dozen. I don't want to talk about this anymore. We have to go to the Bia Sector right away."

She jumped to her feet. But Lien shivered and shook his head.

"I don't want to go back there, and I don't want to fall into Vicra's hands again."

"You're safe now. You're employed by, and under the protection of, my father. They can't do anything else to hurt you."

"I'm still accused of black marketeering."

"No, not even that. Father took care of it."

"That's a real good father you have," he smiled. "I wish I had one like him."

She made a face at him and walked back towards the bungalow. He followed her.

"We haven't eaten yet," he said. "I thought that's why we came here."

She went to a telephone and ordered a picnic basket. Lien was surprised to hear the word, which conjured up images of long gone verdant lawns and small streams.

"There are words that should be banned," he joked. "I can't hear that one without feeling pangs of nostalgia."

"There's another club not too far from here with a rural theme. We could go there and have an old-fashioned picnic, even fish in a river, but it'll have to wait. I want to leave for Bia as soon as we can."

A few minutes later, a servant brought the basket. Floa grabbed it and they went back to her loco-car. Inside, the temperature was closer to the standard seventy degrees, and Lien shivered briefly. He didn't look forward to River Station and its sixty degrees, and sadly looked out at the Tahitian beach.

"We'll come back," promised Floa.

But he didn't entertain too many illusions. They weren't fated to stay together. Everything in life worked to keep them apart, and she would eventually grow bored with him.

Half an hour later, he suddenly realized that they weren't going back to River Station at all, but were instead going directly to the Bia Sector. He was furious.

"Are you crazy? We don't have any equipment with us, not to mention the wolves! What do you think we're going to be able to do?"

"Don't worry," she said. "We have everything we need here. Equipment and guns."

He threw himself down onto a seat and shut his eyes. Floa was being totally unrealistic. She had no idea of what real danger was. She had never suffered from cold, or encountered any real threats in her life. Their little expedition ran a serious risk of ending up as a catastrophe.

"It's no use pretending to be asleep," she said. "I know what you're thinking. You really shouldn't worry so much. I think your stay with Security made you into a bit of a coward."

Lien chose to ignore the rather cruel barb and instead looked outside. Dawn was breaking. Without realizing it, they had spent most of the night at Floa's club.

"Don't they ever sleep there?" he asked.

"They can if they want to, there's room for it. But why would you want to? You come for the warmth, the sand and the water. Hardly anyone ever stays for more than a couple of days anyway. They're all important people, you know..."

He went over to sit next to her. They were passing many other trains, which were now stopped by the priority signals being broadcast from her black box. Their itinerary was electronically sent at least fifteen minutes ahead of their passage, guaranteeing them clear access. At least, that was the theory. If a signal unexpectedly jammed or malfunctioned, they would find themselves on a collision course with an express or a freight train.

"Still a lot of armored convoys," he remarked. "How many new ones do you see every day?"

"I don't know; I stopped counting. It's impressive."

"Do you have any news from the Front?"

"Apparently the war's heating up again. The Siberians are using some kind of rail-missile with a range of more than sixty miles."

"I wonder why they don't fight back with flying missiles."

She looked horrified at his suggestion.

"How can you say that? You know that any non-rail based form of technology is formally prohibited by the C.A.N.Y.S.T."

She meant the Commission for the Application of the New York Station Treaty, the worldwide authority that enforced the Companies' strict adherence to rail, and only rail, as the unique method of travel and locomotion.

"Besides," she added, "I don't think we have the technology anymore to build things that could function at the supercold temperatures of the high atmosphere. We would have to rediscover entire industrial processes, develop new fuels, new alloys..."

Suddenly, he recognized the landscape. They were travelling on Secondary Line 34 and soon, they would reach the junction of S 68 XX.

"Careful. You need to take it from the other direction."

"I know. I read the Guide."

"Which Guide? It wasn't marked in ours."

She showed him a book that she took out of the glove box. He looked at it with curiosity.

"This isn't the one we had. It's much more complete."

"Of course. There are several editions," she explained. "This one is limited to a hundred copies. Some of the lines in it aren't listed in the other Guides. For example, the line we took to go to the club. It's not a good idea for the public to know about places like that. Otherwise any slob with five thousand dollars might want to become a member."

"I take it you're in favor of elitism," he said, his voice heavy with sarcasm.

"Of course. Why should I be stupid enough to feel egalitarian, when I live the kind of life I do."

"You're still threatened by Security, as rich as you may be. Although I still don't understand why they're after you, specifically."

Before answering, Floa switched from electric to steam power. The transition was smooth, but the rhythm of the loco-car changed perceptibly. Lien recognized that he associated the vibration caused by steam with wealth and power. He was quickly becoming enthralled by the promises of what his present relationship with Floa could lead to.

"It's because I'm a woman, and young and beautiful too. They're pigs, especially the high ranking ones. They despise everything that I represent: youth, beauty, freedom. They want to see a sparse, strict military rule. Power supported by severe rationing of all the things that make life enjoyable. Do you know that they have secret connections with the Neo-Catholics?"

She slowed down as they reached the junction with S 68 XX. The switch worked without any glitches, and the loco-car began moving backwards on the abandoned line. Lien felt such a strong emotion that he remained speechless for several minutes. He had no idea of what had happened to his companions Farrell, Lamont, Yann and the others. Major Vicra had told him that they had been freed after informing on him, but he didn't really believe him.

CHAPTER NINE

Lien had no difficulty locating the place where he and his team had installed the temporary line; he easily recognized the shapes of the nearby ice cliffs.

"Everything's gone," Floa said. "The switch, even the tracks themselves. We're going to have to go out and look around."

She went to the rear of the car and came back with an isothermal suit and an odd kind of rifle. Lien had never seen anything like it.

"It's an air gun, made for hunting. It's very effective," she explained.

"Isn't that illegal?"

"I have a special permit. You'd better go alone. If you see any wolves, shoot one and the others will be too busy eating it to bother you."

He went out and waved at her from the outside, then disappeared behind the ice cliffs. In any event, visibility was too restricted for her to hope to keep him in view.

An hour later, in spite of her having signaled loudly several times, he finally returned. When he approached the loco-car, she saw he was carrying two or three large bags.

When he entered the car, she gave him a cup of hot tea and waited for him to speak.

"They're all there, inside my train. The steam engine was taken back to its original position. And inside, I found Farrell, Yann, Lamont... All of them. Frozen to death. Their fuel was gone, and something, or someone, prevented them from leaving. Either the wolves or Security, I don't know. What a horrible death... I brought some things back with me... Vicra told me they'd been pardoned."

She leaned against the control panel, attentively listening to his story.

"Nothing else was missing, except for their isothermal suits," he continued. "They're just all dead. They tried to make a fire with books, files. Hopeless! They were witnesses, just like me. We've got to get away from here right now!"

"Calm down," she said. "You should try to get some more sleep. Go in the cabin, I'll drive."

"We're leaving?"

"No. We're going to try to follow this so-called abandoned line at low speed, as long as we can, anyway. I have a laser rail analyzer. If we keep it down to no more than six to ten miles per hour, there's no risk."

"You're forgetting about Security. What if they're surrounding us? Ready to strike at any minute?"

"Come on, you're in shock. That's normal, considering. Do you want some euphorium?"

"Stuff your drugs! My friends are dead and I'm only alive on a technicality, can you understand that?"

"Yes, but I wouldn't call being under the personal protection of Governor Sadon and his daughter, one of the Trans-European's major stockholders, a technicality. Would you?"

He shrugged.

"Do you really think you're going to be able to stop them?"

"We have a radio link with River Station."

"We had a radio too. They blocked it with some kind of electro-magnetic field."

"They wouldn't dare attack me," she said sharply. "I want to know why two abnormally long trains secretly travelled this line."

Trying to forget the grim sight of his friends' bodies, Lien didn't argue with her. Later, as they moved along the edge of an impressive glacier, he began to study the Railway Guide.

"We should come out onto some kind of plateau, but there's a four percent uphill gradient."

"No problem. This car is equipped with electro-magnets."

The results of the rail analyzer appeared on a small monitor screen. The line itself was old, but still in reasonably good condition, at least in most places. There were areas where the soldered joints were cracked, but for a loco-car as small as the one they were using, it wasn't a problem.

"It looks like we should come to a bridge crossing some kind of canyon soon. It might have collapsed."

"We've got to stop," she said in a strange, low voice.

He looked up and saw the Redfurs. There were at least a hundred of them and, for the first time in his life, he saw their women. He was struck by their wild beauty. In spite of the fur that covered their bodies, one could see the shape of their breasts and admire their lithe, muscled forms. It was as if the Ice People never aged or became decrepit.

"I think we might have a problem," she said.

"Why don't you back up?"

With her head, she indicated the screen that monitored the back of the car. The Ice People had caused a huge block of ice to collapse on the rails, like the Indians used to do to wagon trains in the old westerns.

"Do you think they're acting on orders from Security?"

"Frankly, right now, I couldn't care less," Floa replied curtly. "I can clear behind us with our laser, but it's going to take awhile. If they attack us in the meantime, it won't take long for them to break in. Did you notice what they're carrying?"

Lien looked again and jumped. The Redfurs were carrying shovels, axes, picks, iron bars, all tools that obviously belonged to the Company, and which were part of every loco's tool kit.

"That's really strange. They must have looted a train."

Suddenly, one of the Redfurs approached the airlock door and knocked twice on the glass window. He was an athletic giant, but Lien saw no hate or anger in his eyes. He said as much to Floa, who didn't share his opinion.

"They're animals. A beast doesn't necessarily look fierce when it's eating its prey. I don't trust him."

"But when we were with your friends the Outsiders, there was a Redfur there and..."

"Only one, and he was civilized. These are wild."

Suddenly, she screamed, pointing at the screen again.

"There. Look!"

The screen showed an Ice Woman who had moved closer to the car, perhaps spurred on by curiosity.

"Look what she has around her neck!" Floa said.

She was wearing a metal chain with a small badge on which there were two metal letters held together by a small metal bar: F-S.

"F Station!" Floa said, her eyes wide in horror.

"What do you mean, F Station?"

"Don't you remember? The night we met, that was the city they were sending into exile. We drove alongside it. It took up almost a hundred lines..."

"Yes, but..."

"The people onboard had been ordered to wear this badge. Can't you see?"

"This woman isn't the only one wearing it," Lien said, almost thinking aloud. "They all have them."

By then, the Ice Man at the door was getting impatient, and his knocks had become more forceful. He was shouting things that they couldn't hear through the airlock, but which sounded demanding.

"We've got to do something," Floa said, "otherwise he'll try to break in."

"I'll go out and see what he wants," Lien said.

Once again he put on his isothermal suit and walked into the lock; he hesitated for one or two seconds before he had the courage to open the outer door. The Ice Man had stepped back down onto the ice; Lien followed him. He had considered staying on the steps in order to remain at the same height as the giant, but had rejected the idea.

They looked at each other for a few seconds, then the Redfur took Lien's arm, but immediately released it with a frown of disgust. Obviously, he didn't like the feel of the isothermal suit. Instead, he indicated that Lien should follow him.

Lien did so, walking past a group of Ice Women who were looking at him brazenly. One of them stepped in front of him and touched his groin as if trying to discover whether there was a man inside the suit. He thought, not without fear, that if the suit had had an opening there, and she had found it and opened it, he wouldn't have stayed a man very long with the ambient temperature of minus eighty degrees Fahrenheit!

Eventually, she found his manhood and said something aloud that he didn't understand, but which made all the others laugh. He had never felt so humiliated in his entire life.

He ran to catch up with his guide, who was leading him along the ice-encrusted rails of the line. It had taken all the modern equipment contained in Floa's loco-car to travel on such tracks.

Then, they arrived at the collapsed bridge; it was so old that its deck had totally crumbled into the gaping crevice. This was, quite literally, the end of the line. It was impossible to go further. Lien was afraid of having an attack of vertigo, and didn't dare get near the edge of the cliff, but the Ice Man shouted something at him, and gestured for him to come closer. So, he took some careful steps forward, while trying very hard not to look down.

Suddenly, he noticed that the Redfurs had dug steps in the side of the ice cliff, and his guide motioned that Lien should follow him down. The path looked as if it had been well-travelled, and as they descended, they continually passed numerous other Ice People, including women and children, going in the opposite direction, their arms full of amazing artifacts: pieces of clothing, furniture, tools, books, fabrics, and food. Huge quantities of food.

The descent took a full half-hour, during which Lien kept his eyes mostly glued to the back of his guide, not daring to confront the edge of the cliff. He didn't know how deep they were inside the ice, but he didn't feel like trying to reach an estimate by looking into the canyon itself. It took the noise of a crowd to tell him that they had at last reached the bottom.

He had never seen so many Redfurs gathered in a single place; even on the dome of Grand Star Station there were less. This tribe must have numbered over five hundred. There were many children, some able to walk, others, still too young, were carried in their mothers' arms. They seemed well-fed, although it was possible that their fur could hide an emaciated body. He noticed one of the children licking a milk popsicle with a gluttonous expression on his face. Another was burying his face in a container of powdered sugar.

Now that he could look around without worrying about vertigo, he took his time. He saw an incredible pile of crushed railcars, their metallic frames broken and mingling with one another, making a giant scrapheap of unprecedented height. These weren't the railcars of a normal express or omnibus train, but the larger residential type that made up the smaller cities, like F Station. Some cars had even been designed with a certain architectural look in mind: neo-gothic or in imitation of the alpine style.

He remembered the metallic badges worn by the Ice People, and, looking at the demolished cars, he knew at once that this was indeed F Station -- or at least, part of it. At first, he thought that Security had dumped the railcars into this canyon as an additional form of punishment for the most dangerous of the rebels, depriving them of their homes, then carting them away to rot in concentration camps.

But, as he walked over a natural ice bridge, he saw the first bodies. The Ice People had lined them up in an even configuration in a corner of the canyon. They made almost perfect pyramids: the men on one side, the women on another, and the children in the middle.

He had to stop, and lean against the icy walls; around him, the Redfurs walked by, oblivious to his presence. He couldn't move, struck by the horror. He tried to count the bodies, but couldn't, there were too many; his mind grew numb. His guide soon realized that he was no longer following him and returned.

"Come," he said.

Lien Rag received another shock, which was enough to draw him out of his stupor.

"You know our language?"

"Come."

Soon they were walking away from the macabre pyramids, although several times Lien turned his head to look at them again, as if to convince himself of their reality. They had reached a sort of first level, dug inside the cliff. That's where the crushed railcars were the most numerous. Lien guessed that the huge crevice must have continued on, growing ever more narrow, but it had undoubtedly been filled by the first of the two convoys. Two trains of about three miles in length between them. Dozens and dozens of cars, thousands of people. Security had dealt with the most dangerous elements in F Station, by sending them crashing to their deaths in this abyss, while quietly deporting the rest.

"There," the Ice Man said.

He seemed terror-stricken, and Lien quickly understood the reason.

Lying on its side, a massive, old, half-broken steam engine was still operating. He was familiar with this type, which was about two hundred years old; its water was heated by the combustion of radioactive waste. He stepped back, trying to pull the Ice Man away, but the latter refused to budge.

"No... You come... Stop..."

It was a very old machine that had probably been repaired many times during its life. The radioactive material was locked inside a container made of lead and iron that, in theory, was supposed to be airtight, but leaks were frequent. It warmed the water of a tubular turbo-engine, which in turn transmitted the energy to a series of old-fashioned pistons. The frequent breakdowns in these machines had eventually led the Company to retire them and, from what he had heard, bury them in a deep ice cavern, so as to avoid any problems with the radioactivity. Obviously, Security had rescued these two for one last, deadly ride.

"Very dangerous," Lien tried to explain. "Very dangerous. We have to go."

"You come. Stop it."

What must have been the most frightening to him, Lien thought, was the loud huffing of the steam engine which, in spite of the fall, was still operating. The hot water leaked from various cracks, congealing almost immediately into vapor, then ice. It was radioactive, of course, and Lien didn't seem to be able to convince the Ice Man that getting near it meant death.

"Stop. Quick."

"No, you have to leave, all of you," Lien said, making large gestures with his arm. "This is bad. It can explode."

It was likely that this tribe of Ice People had never come near the Company's networks, and had, therefore, never seen its mightiest engines. They had spent all their lives in this deadly cold area, for the most part far from men and his technology. Normally, he would have expected them to be completely ignorant of their very existence. Yet, this Ice Man knew some words of man's language, which he must have learned during brief contacts with traders or other civilized people.

While looking at the remains of the engine, Lien tried to imagine how the tribe must have reacted on the night when the two trains had been launched into the void at full speed. Yet, they had managed to overcome their fear to approach the wrecks, which they had then looted.

A Redfur woman approached them, carrying cans of food. She showed them to the Ice Man, who sniffed them suspiciously.

"They're okay," Lien said. "Good."

He took one and pulled it open; it contained meatballs with soja sauce. He conspicuously pretended to eat it, to show them. Immediately, the woman grabbed back the can and ate its entire contents in seconds.

Suddenly, the Ice Man grabbed Lien by his shoulders and pushed him towards the wreck. Seeing that Lien refused to move forward, he grabbed a piece of steel and used it as a prod. Several children, drawn to the scene, began to pelt the engineer with debris.

"Listen," he tried to plead. "It's radioactive. Even the steam is dangerous..."

But he had to give in, or risk being pelted to death by the Redfurs. He made an attempt to hide behind the carcass of a railcar, but the children quickly dislodged him. He had no choice but to walk towards the smoking wreck. Not only was he risking radioactive contamination, and a slow, painful death in the process, but he could also be scolded by an unexpected jet of boiling steam.

Indeed, such a burst occurred, missing him by only a few inches, which caused him to jump and made the children laugh. He stepped into the remains of the control booth to look for a safety valve that would empty the turbine's water into some kind of container, or failing that, outside. He knew it wouldn't solve the problem of the radioactivity, but at least, the engine would stop running, and the Redfurs would let him go.

He tried to remember what he had learned about these old engines in college, but at first he was unable to think of anything at all. Then, he recalled something about an autonomous water supply valve that recycled the water into the turbine. If he could find it and close it, it would effectively shut down the engine.

It was easier than he had thought it would be. The water supply system had broken open under the shock, and it was the ice melted by the engine's heat which kept it running. Once he had located the system, it was child's play to shut it down. He them waited patiently for the engine to run out of water.

Soon, the steam bursts grew weaker and, eventually, stopped. Running out of steam, the turbine began winding down. Lien was struck with the fear that it might explode, so he left in a hurry, preferring to face the Ice Children than to remain trapped inside the dying engine.

CHAPTER TEN

Amused in spite of the situation, Floa tested Lien with a Geiger counter after he had taken a shower.

"Tiny traces of radioactivity, but nothing to worry about," she said. "You were really scared, weren't you?"

"Are they still out there?" he asked, annoyed by her condescending attitude.

"Yes. I'm worried that they might decide to use us to do all the dirty jobs they're afraid of doing. Now that you've turned off that engine, they probably think you're a great wizard or something."

"Cut it out!"

The turbine hadn't exploded and the Redfurs had allowed him to walk out of the canyon and return to the railcar. But he couldn't get the image of the pyramids of frozen bodies out of his mind.

"It was F Station's rebel leaders and their families. There must have been hundreds of them, maybe thousands."

"Now we know how Security takes care of that kind of problem. I bet the Board will be happy to find out."

"Maybe they already know."

"Impossible. I would have been told," she replied curtly. "I have to get down there and take pictures."

"The Redfurs may not let you. And it might be dangerous."

"Are you afraid they'll rape me?" she said with a weird undercurrent in her voice that made him wonder.

"I did see that female fondling you before, you know. I thought she was going to rape you, but then, I wonder if you could perform, knowing what exposure to the outside air would do to you."

He left her to her thoughts and went to the back of the car to make himself a sandwich. He ate without really tasting his food, and drank a beer. Eventually, Floa joined him and kissed him tenderly, almost like a peace offering.

"You're right, I was being silly. We're wasting fuel. If they don't let us go, we'll be dead in two days. We have two choices: we can try to force our way out, which will be risky, or I can radio for help. Security will rescue us, but it'll be extremely humiliating for me and my father."

"The only way to force our way out is to use the laser. That will kill them."

"So?"

"I don't want to kill anyone."

"Don't be stupid," she replied. "Would you prefer us to die?"

"I'm sure we can negotiate something with them. I found out the name of the one who led me before. It's Noo. He didn't seem unsympathetic to me."

"Like when he let their brats throw stones at you?"

"I don't think he had any choice then. Anyway, that's all behind us now."

The Ice People kept watch over the railcar from a distance, being sure not to lose it from sight.

"They're nothing but looters," she said.

"They took advantage of an opportunity, they didn't create it. If you call Security, they'll come, but then, they'll try to get rid of us. I'm sure of that..."

He raised his hand to forestall her obvious objection.

"... I know that you're an important person, but important people die in accidents every day, too. Once you and I are dead, who cares what your father will do to Security. No, we've got to get out of this by ourselves."

Nothing happened until late afternoon when, suddenly, Floa spotted a man wearing a black isothermal suit with an embroidered silver cross on the back. Immediately she called Lien to the window.

"It's a Neo-Catholic missionary!"

"You know those people?"

"Father authorized them to preach in our District. Those people, as you put it, are more and more important every day."

"I wonder what he's doing here?"

"They've decided to convert the Redfurs and teach them our language. These savages are ready to believe in anything. I've heard that the ones who work on our domes think we're gods, living inside an ice bubble. And they're amazed that we can move through the ice so easily."

"Some of them must have gotten used to it, because I never had the feeling that I was being worshiped by the ones at Grand Star Station."

Floa didn't answer, and turned back towards the window. She was angry that the missionary didn't come directly to them. Instead, he went from one group of Ice People to another, tapping them on their shoulders, patting the heads of the children. He didn't even seem interested in the loco-car.

"He'll have to come to us eventually. He'll just have to," Floa said, tensely.

"How did he get here in the first place?"

"I don't know. With a sled, maybe? They're allowed to use them for their long-range missions."

"They're really being coddled," Lien said, instinctively wary of anything connected with religion and politics.

Eventually, Floa turned her back to the window in exasperation.

"Let's go and make love," she said.

"But what if this guy wants to see us?"

"Fine. Then we can invite him in."

While Lien had been outside with the Redfurs, she had changed into a jumpsuit. She undid its fastenings, exposing the fact that she was completely naked underneath. Lien cast a last glance towards the missionary before following her to the back of the car. But, suddenly, he stopped, paled, and almost vomited. Floa immediately understood his delayed nervous reaction.

"I thought I was going to get you to forget everything you saw down there, but I guess it's not going to work after all."

Lien shook his head. In his mind, he still saw the pyramids of frozen bodies. She went into the cabin and came back with a bottle of vodka and a glass.

"Drink this; it'll do you some good."

He took the glass and downed it. She refilled it. Suddenly, he caught something out of the corner of his eye.

"The priest is coming," he said.

Behind the Plexiglas of the man's hood, he could see a clean-shaven face. Somehow, he was surprised. He had expected him to be bearded. The missionary gestured at them to open the airlock, entered it, and a few seconds later, stepped into the cabin removing his hood.

"Well, I certainly wasn't expecting to find anyone in such a lonely spot. What are you two doing here?"

"We came to find out about the two convoys. The ones that fell into the canyon."

"Reporters?" he inquired suspiciously.

"No," Lien answered, without volunteering any other information. "Did you see the remains there? The bodies?"

"I wouldn't mind a glass of what you're holding," the missionary said. "And yes, I did see the wreck, and those abominable pyramids of corpses. But I don't know what it's all about..."

"It's a crime, committed by Security."

"By the way, my name's Peter. You can call me Brother Peter. I'm not sure I agree with you, you know. It seems to me that it must be a very ancient tragedy. The type of engine that pulled the train was quite old."

"How can you say that?" Lien said, enraged. "It was still smoking a couple of hours ago. I had to shut it down myself. In fact, one of them, Noo, forced me to do it."

"Ah, yes, Noo... A good man and a wonderful leader."

"Did you hear what I said?" Lien shouted. "There was steam! Those bodies are no more than a couple of days old!"

Brother Peter looked at Floa and smiled.

"I understand your friend's reaction... Your husband?"

"No, just a friend."

Lien wondered how she could keep to her cool tone and not get indignant.

"I went down there and prayed for the souls of those poor people."

"While you were there, did you happen to notice what the Ice People were wearing around their necks?

The "F-S" badges? Although I don't suppose you heard about the entire town being exiled because it had rebelled against the Company? Those two trains came from that town, they weren't just ordinary trains; they were from F Station. But you wouldn't know anything about that, would you?"

"Please, don't say things like that," Brother Peter said softly. "I don't know what those metal badges mean, but I can assure you that the wreck is at least two hundred years old. The cold preserves things perfectly, you know. You must have been mistaken."

Lien looked at Floa who was warming her drink with her hands, seemingly completely uninterested by the conversation. Too uninterested to be convincing, in fact. Was it her way of signaling him to drop the subject, and be careful of what he said to the priest?

"No, in my opinion," Brother Peter continued, "this is a very old train. I'm not saying that you didn't see what you saw, but the fact that the engine was still working after such a long time isn't all that surprising. Those nuclear-powered machines could run for years. And the steam came from the melted ice. You see, it's really quite simple after all."

Lien had trouble remaining calm. Brother Peter was lying with such conviction that he understood it was not a story improvised on the spot, but a clever, carefully rehearsed distortion of the facts. Put in such a light, what he had seen could, indeed, be thus explained.

"If you shut down that reactor, you did a service to those poor people out there. You should be proud."

Noo had forced him to do it. Now, Lien wondered if, perhaps, Brother Peter wasn't behind it all. A wreck that continued to operate would raise more questions than one which no longer functioned.

"It was a horrible accident," the priest continued. "But I'm sure that if one was to look in the archives, one would find records of it. The first train must have weakened the bridge, so that it collapsed when the second attempted to cross. That's why this line was catalogued XX. I'm sure that the sight of all those bodies must have shaken you more than you realize."

Lien thought how ironic it was that Major Vicra had called him mad, and now the priest was saying he was mentally unbalanced. He made a last, half-hearted attempt.

"Listen, I was in this area a week ago, I'm a Glaciologist. I was with my team, and we had very accurate scientific instruments with us. One night, we registered the passage of two trains on our seismograph; two very long trains. Two trains which were amazingly similar to the ones lying down there now. How do you explain that?"

Brother Peter looked at Floa very briefly. They exchanged a glance that Lien caught.

"No, I'm not crazy, if that's what you're wondering," he said sarcastically.

"Of course, of course. Your story is certainly extremely mysterious. Are you positive your equipment just didn't register an ice quake? They're quite frequent in this area, you know."

"I showed the tapes to Major Vicra of Security, but now they seem to have disappeared, and my men are all dead."

As he said it, he realized that he no longer had any tangible evidence; there was nothing he could prove. Even the piles of bodies could be explained away as Brother Peter had done, and if not, Security probably wouldn't hesitate to blast the canyon shut, burying all traces of its crimes under tons of ice.

"I see, I see," Brother Peter said in the same tone of voice that he must use with children, or Ice People.

Lien stood up, and went to the window. He saw an Ice Woman breast feeding a strong, vigorous looking baby. She looked at him briefly, without expressing any emotion.

"Did you come here to try converting them?" Lien asked, changing the subject.

"It's not that simple," replied the missionary. "First, the Council of New Rome must decide whether or not they have souls. We know nothing about their origins. If it turns out that they're animals, it would be sacrilegious to try to instruct them in the word of our Lord. Meanwhile, we're encouraged to visit them to try to alleviate their sufferings."

"They're unaware of the worse kind of suffering," Lien shrugged. "The cold."

Outside, the Ice Woman was still feeding her child. Lien could see the tip of her breast, which made a pink spot on her reddish fur. Involuntarily, his eyes glanced lower at her pubic area, which was covered by darker fur.

"They are lost," the priest, suddenly very close to him, whispered.

Lien was startled, because he hadn't heard him move.

"I find them very beautiful," he said.

"They're just animals," Brother Peter said in a strange, fanatical, tone of voice. "Nothing but animals. Their seduction is an act of the devil. They can put thoughts of fornication into people's minds, but they are sinful thoughts. It would be like lusting after a goat, or a reindeer."

Suddenly, it occurred to Lien that the priest had spent much time alone with the Redfurs and must have often been subject to temptation. He couldn't repress a smile.

"I find them beautiful too," Floa said, joining them. "I understand why there are men and women who are sexually attracted to them."

"Please, do not say these things," the missionary said, perspiring profusely.

Maybe he was hot from being inside the warm cabin of the loco-car, even though his isothermal suit was mostly open.

"They don't want to let us leave," Floa said suddenly. "They blocked the way with huge chunks of ice. We could cut our way through with our laser, but we don't want to kill any of them by accident. Can you help us?"

Brother Peter remained silent for a few seconds, still looking at the nursing woman.

"I know of a few children born from such misalliances," he said. "Oh, not in our society, because there, it's easy to get an abortion. But out here, I've seen bastard children, suffering because of their condition. Their fathers gave them a certain form of intelligence, when the only thing they truly needed was the ability to withstand cold. Because of their low resistance, they suffer and are scoffed at by the others. In the end, they have no choice but to exile themselves from their tribes and, more often than not, they die alone in the wilderness."

Then, he shook his head as if to clear it of his daydreams, and answered Floa's question.

"I don't know why Noo is keeping you here. He said nothing about it to me. Normally, we don't like to intervene in their affairs."

"You mean to say that you're not going to help us," Lien said, growing irritated again.

"I didn't say that, but I must act carefully. Be patient."

"We can't wait too long, or else we'll run out of fuel," Floa said.

"I'm not going far. I won't abandon you."

He left the loco-car, and they saw him walk along the rails towards the canyon where the Redfurs had gathered.

"He knows very well that those two trains were wrecked recently," Lien said furious.

"Yes, he does," Floa replied, "But what you don't know is that the Neo-Catholic Church is behind Security's stock buying program."

CHAPTER ELEVEN

It was an exhausting night; neither Lien nor Floa were able to sleep. They had decided to keep their iso-thermal suits on, in case of an attack, but at the same time, it was impossible to lower the temperature inside the loco-car without damaging some of its sensitive in-struments. As a result, they were too hot. Once in a while, one of them went to the window to take a look outside.

"That priest obviously just wrote us off," Lien said. "He's not about to take the least risk on our behalf."

"Unless he's busy screwing one of their females. You saw how he looked when he talked about it. And his little speech about poor, suffering half-breeds smacked of personal guilt to me."

They drank vodka to help pass the time, and soon the sweet smell of alcohol permeated the cabin.

"If they refuse to let us go, I can try to reach my fa-ther and explain the situation. But Security will probably intercept my message because he doesn't normally get coded communications..."

Finally, dawn came. When they looked outside, they noticed that the Ice People had gone, leaving noth-ing behind but a small amount of garbage. Floa ran hap-pily from one window to the other.

"This time, it looks like they're gone for good. I can laser through the ice blocks and we'll be out of here within minutes."

"What about your pictures?"

"What pictures?"

"The ones you wanted to take down below, show-ing all the bodies."

"I'm going to forget about it," she said vehemently. "Didn't you hear what the priest said? We've both got to forget about all of it. Especially me, for the good of the Company."

"For the good of the Company," Lien repeated sarcastically. "Security murdered a couple of thousand people, including my friends..."

Suddenly, he grabbed her camera and walked towards the airlock.

"Lien!"

He locked the inner door, to prevent her from stopping him.

"Lien! Come back here!"

He stepped outside, and walked towards the canyon. Floa appeared behind him, and shouted from the top of the metal steps.

"Come back! I won't wait for you!"

Then, she walked back inside and blew the air horn for awhile. Finally, she used the loudspeaker. Her voice must have carried for miles.

"Listen to me! If you don't come back right this minute, I'll drive away. I swear I will. I'm fed up with all this shit!"

She continued to shout at him, sometimes threatening, sometimes begging. He reached the edge of the huge chasm and looked for the steps that he had taken with the Redfurs, but found no trace of them. Finally, he lay on the ground and, fighting his vertigo, looked down into the abyss. The path was still there, but now began thirty feet below the edge of the cliff. The Redfurs had used their tools to destroy the top of the path. He estimated that it would take at least a day to dig a new one. Then, it occurred to him that Floa's loco-car was equipped with a winding drum and chains. If they moved it closer to the edge, Floa could lower him to where the path began, and from there he could walk safely to the bottom. He felt he could control his fear of heights long enough to take the necessary photos.

He walked back to the loco-car. The wind had risen and was blowing hard enough to force him to lower his head, so, it was only when he actually reached the spot where the loco-car had been that he noticed it was gone; Floa hadn't been bluffing. She had cut the ice blocks into small chunks with her laser, and then had used the loco's fenders to sweep the pieces away.

He wasn't really surprised by her actions, he admitted to himself. She had finally figured out where her personal interest lay. The Company couldn't be accused of mass murder, and since she, too, was part of the Company, she could not afford open conflict with her own kind. She liked her way of life, with its privileges and comforts too much; she couldn't bear to be without them. By abandoning him here, she also abandoned the permanent reminder of guilt that he would always have symbolized for her in the future. She may even have been abandoning a certain form of romantic love that he had come to represent. Their kind of passion implied a sharing and commitment that she must have thought burdensome, in comparison to her usual sexual dalliances.

Instead of giving up, he walked along the rails in the direction of the Secondary line. He had just trekked along the entire distance of the three-thousand foot long glacier, when, just beyond it, he saw the loco-car. She must have forgotten to totally shut down the steam valve because it was making a regular, and reassuring, puffing noise, waiting peacefully just after a particularly sharp curve in the line. Suddenly, he was filled with hope and happiness. He too wanted to have a comfortable and carefree life, and enjoy the benefits of his position, but he would never admit that to her. Never.

"Give it to me," she said.

She was standing outside, waiting for him. She held her hand out towards the camera, but he refused.

"Don't be a fool," she said.

"What do you want to do with it? Embarrass Security?"

"Give it to me."

"No. Brother Peter's words made you think. You know where your interest lies now. The need to cover up for the Company is too strong for you to fight."

"Don't argue with me; give me that camera."

She took her air rifle and aimed it at him.

"Would you really shoot me?"

"Yes."

"In that case, I yield to force. But first, look!"

She made a quizzical face as he laughed and opened the camera. It was empty.

"You didn't take any pictures?"

"I couldn't. They'd destroyed the path."

Suddenly, she laughed too, and threw him the gun.

"What a pair we make. That's not loaded either. We're equal now."

"Are you happy about it."

"No, but I want to live. Everyone back there is dead, and so are your friends. We're not. We're alive. In this icy world you need to be tough to survive. But I won't forget this; someday, I'll get my revenge. I think the trains must have been controlled by remote, by the way."

Suddenly Lien had a revelation.

"The electro-magnetic screen. The Faraday cage. They repowered the line just for that one night, so that the automatic guidance mechanisms on those old engines could function. It was obviously at an extremely high tension. That's why our radio didn't work."

They began their slow drive back. As they passed Lien's old train, he remarked, "An icy shroud for a team of Glaciologists. Somehow, it seems kind of appropriate."

They had been driving for hours, when he asked her where they were going. She told him that she had to get back to River Station. Earlier, along the Secondary Line, she had made a stop to refuel the engine and call her father.

"I'd rather go back to the Club," he said.

"We can go there afterwards."

"What does your father want?"

She seemed uncomfortable, and didn't answer. He understood.

"He doesn't like you being with me. Maybe he thinks your latest fancy is lasting too long?"

"Not quite, but he wants to see you. You know that he always worries about me, because of the shares I inherited from my maternal grandfather. He thinks, and rightfully so, that it exposes me to all kinds of danger."

"Including fortune hunters?"

"Don't worry about that. He's pretty open-minded."

"Even when it comes to us?" Lien said testily.

She tried to kiss him, but he shied away.

"I don't want to marry you, you know. I have a job and I'd like to go back to it. I hope I'll get another assignment when all this dies down."

"Don't talk to me like that. I can do whatever I want, and I'd like you to live with me, that's all."

"Have you considered the fact that maybe I'm not cut out for a life of being idly comfortable?"

"If that's true, why are you so eager to get back to the Club ?"

That compelling need to forget one's daily worries, to live in total luxury for two hours, maybe even two days -- was it already a step towards compromise, towards learning to live like the idle rich? He knew she believed that he could learn to live like that and enjoy it, but she didn't know the forces inside that drove him. He would never be able to settle for such an existence on a permanent basis.

"I've got you there, don't I?" she laughed.

He decided not to argue the point; she would never understand.

"You sure do!"

When they arrived at River Station, they were immediately switched to a priority line leading directly to the Governor's palace. Lien saw the other travelers looking at them enviously, and understood how they felt. On the outer surface of the dome, the Ice People were cleaning away the snow and ice that never stopped falling. He could barely see their silhouettes behind the milky white glass. He thought about Noo and his tribe wandering endlessly in the wilderness and wondered if the Siberians used Ice People too. He asked Floa, but her mind was on her driving, and she distractedly told him that she had never thought about it, but that they probably did.

For a minute, he envied the lives of these creatures, the only ones who were free to roam the planet, without paying attention to the conflicts of man.

"Your father must have quite a library, I guess?"

"Yes. A huge one, as a matter of fact."

He was happy to hear it. He wanted to look up all the books written about the Redfurs, and try to fathom the secret of their origins. Suddenly, the loco-car stopped.

"Terminus," Floa said, smiling. "We're going to see my dear Daddy. He must have been terribly worried."

CHAPTER TWELVE

"Aren't you dressed yet?"

Floa had burst into the palace's library. Lien was reading, but he jumped as if he had been caught doing something wrong, and rubbed his eyes. The young woman had turned on the powerful ceiling chandelier, although Lien had been happy just to use a desk lamp.

"I'm sorry. I got caught up in this book."

She took it, almost ripping it out of his hands, read the title and shrugged.

"*Two Years Among the Ice People*, by Gregor Lukas. What is it, another one of your stupid, old history books?"

"Not so old, and don't lose my place. It was only written about fifty years ago. Lukas made some startling discoveries about the Redfurs, and I'm amazed that no one took any notice. The book's almost totally forgotten now."

She shook her head, took his hand and dragged him towards the elevator that led to their personal apartment. They had a huge living room, and an even more impressive bathroom, with a bathtub as big as a swimming pool. But there were two separate bedrooms, as the Governor insisted that they sleep in separate beds until their marriage, which would only take place in three months.

Lien had taken back his book and began quoting from it.

"For instance, he studied their basal metabolism, which is very different from ours. It can withstand extremely low temperatures. Of course, our metabolism has changed a bit since the beginning of the ice age..."

Floa nodded as if she was paying attention to what he was saying, but, in fact, was concentrating more on removing his clothes in order to get him dressed for the party they were supposed to attend.

"... We've gotten used to living in temperatures below 40 degrees. It's only in places like your Club that we're suddenly confronted with pre-ice age temperatures...:

He smiled when Floa began teasing him through his underclothes. He loved the sexy playfulness she displayed in their daily lives.

"Do we have time before the party?" he asked.

She smiled back.

"No, I'm afraid we don't. We're late enough as it is."

"I'm going to be turned on all night. I'll probably grab hold of the first woman I see."

"You can always try General Harris' wife," she smiled. "I've noticed the way she always looks at you."

"She's too fat and snobbish for my taste... But going back to Gregor Lukas, he was an exceptional man..."

"Who?"

"Gregor Lukas. The man who lived among the Red-furs!"

Annoyed by her indifference, he pushed her aside and finished dressing by himself. He found the latest fashion in clothes rather ridiculous: loose pants tucked into leather boots, a red and green embroidered tunic, and a Cossack-like fur hat. Floa was wearing a similar tunic, going down to her knees, but no pants. The tunic was slit up to her hips on one side, and she wasn't wearing anything underneath.

"It's more naughty than actually indecent," he had remarked when she had asked his opinion. Now, he was reminded that the style of the clothes looked like pictures of the festive clothes worn by the Lapps, a cultural tribe from the pre-ice age days.

"Have you ever heard of the Lapps?" he asked. "I think they've been completely assimilated for centuries..."

"I may have read something about them once. Why?"

"What if the Redfurs were their descendents? No, that doesn't make any sense..."

In the loco-car on the way to the party, she finally had enough, and berated him both for spending more time in the library than with her, and for what she perceived to be an unhealthy obsession with the Ice People.

"We've been here a month and we've barely gone out!"

"That's not true. We went to the Club several times."

"There are other places to go besides the Club; cabarets, for example. I love cabarets, and there are some really good ones that stop here on a regular basis. Last time I went, I saw a terrific transvestite number, and you refused to come with me."

"I hate that kind of show."

"You're prejudiced. I'd never have dreamed that you'd turn into a bookworm."

"I'm sorry," he said, suddenly sincere. "I didn't mean to make your life difficult."

The Governor, his future father-in-law, had managed to get him a leave of absence with pay, under the pretense that he was writing a scientific report on the changes in the Seventeenth District's ice structure. In reality, he was spending most of his time researching the Redfurs, and had already discovered a dozen books dealing with the subject, without, however, finding any more clues about their origins.

Floa was touched by his apologies and pulled him towards her. They kissed passionately. Lien's hand crept up under her tunic and began caressing the young woman. She leaned back and nibbled his ear.

"I'll accept this as an advance against tonight, in case we come back late and are tired."

But instead of concentrating on his companion's pleasure, Lien let his thoughts wander to the outside wilderness, where tribes of Ice People wandered endlessly. Floa's brief orgasm shook him back to reality.

"You haven't been paying attention," she said at last. "To punish you, I won't take care of you tonight. You'll have to wait until tomorrow... or do it yourself!"

"You're colder than the ice," he said smiling.

Floa always timed her arrival at parties to be an event. This time was no different. As always, she was the most beautiful woman in the room, and when a valet helped her take off her fur coat, her new dress stunned the crowd.

Later, Lien found himself at the bar, drinking a mixture of vodka and fruit juice. Although fruit was a rare commodity for ordinary people, the Company's rich executives could afford to have it grown under controlled conditions. There were special luxury shops which catered to these people, stocking delicacies that had not otherwise been seen since the ice age began.

"Are you Glaciologist Lien Rag?"

A small man wearing glasses, and an outrageous embroidered jacket which was much too big for his frail shape, had walked over to him.

"I remember meeting you once at a scientific symposium on tertiary ice flows and their impact on environing life forms. It was at Merkur Station, three years ago. My name is Hal Mern."

"Of course! I remember you perfectly," Lien said, suddenly no longer bored. "You gave a paper on new species... Wolves and other ice predators. You were supposed to talk about the Redfurs, but somehow, that item got cancelled for a security reason of some kind."

Hal Mern looked around the room suspiciously.

"Yes, they said that they expected a demonstration the next day, and used it as an excuse to cancel my speech. Later, I learned by accident that there was no demonstration. It had all been a lie to keep me from talking."

Lien suddenly wondered if this really was a chance encounter. He began to worry. His recent interest in the Ice People must have become known; could it be that they were sending Hal Mern to find out what he knew?

"But maybe this isn't a good place to talk about it," Mern continued.

Was he sincere, Lien wondered, or was this just another trick to inspire his confidence, and extract information. He decided it would be best to remain on his guard.

"Do you know what I've become since? A zoo keeper! Guardian of a few miserable animals; travelling from town to town. I'm in River Station tonight only because it was the next stop on my schedule..."

Then, he added, as if to assuage Lien's unspoken suspicions.

"I think the only reason I got invited here tonight was because General Harris's wife loves animals."

"You don't study the new ice age species any-more?" asked Lien.

"No. You need time and money for that. I no longer have either. My work on the Redfurs was stopped too. The Academy said it didn't belong in the field of zoology, which I knew of course, but I needed a convenient label. And, since we no longer study Anthropology... But in spite of all their efforts to stop me, I've perse-vered. I've even managed to gain access to a number of books and documents during my travels..."

He took one of the short, greenish cigars nicknamed nibs, which had a slight, euphoric effect. He offered one to Lien, but the Glaciologist refused. When Mern lit his nib, Lien noticed his hand was shaking.

"Are you interested in the Redfurs too?" he asked in a low voice.

"Well, I have given some thought to the subject," Lien answered, noncommittally.

"Have you ever met any? Not many people have. And yet, there are so many of them living just above our heads. But those aren't the ones that are really interest-ing to study. By living in such proximity to our society, they've lost their true, cultural identity. The interesting ones are those who continue to live in nomadic tribes."

"The ones Gregor Lukas lived with," Lien said, immediately regretting his outburst. If Mern really was a Company spy, he would realize that Lien's interest went beyond the casual. But Mern grabbed his arm with a strength that was surprising for such a frail individual.

"Lukas? You know about Lukas?"

"I read his book."

"Two Years Among The Ice People. It's almost im-possible to find. I've only seen photocopies of excerpts, and those were in terrible condition."

"The book is in the Governor's library, at the palace."

"You have access to the Governor's library?" Mern asked, suddenly frightened.

"Well, I'm a friend of the family and..."

"I'm very happy for you. Very happy," the little man said abruptly. "I see someone I know. I must go and say hello. Excuse me."

Lien was taken aback by this unexpected departure. He followed the small silhouette with his eyes, and in fact, saw Mern leave the party altogether. He decided to act, and rushed towards the exit, bumping into several people and apologizing on the run.

He caught up with the scientist as he was getting an old, tattered coat from a supercilious valet.

"Wait. We've barely had a chance to talk."

"I must go. I assure you..."

"Let me come with you then."

He asked for his coat and chased after the zoologist, who had already gone outside. They walked along the deserted platforms in silence, crossing a row of wheel-mounted military barracks, then came to a middle-class residential area composed of small dwelling units, which were also on wheels. Some of the poorest families were only entitled to cars with 6 square feet of usable space per person, with collective bathrooms and kitchens, and often, inadequate heating systems.

"Listen, Mern, just because I'm engaged to the Governor's daughter doesn't mean I'm going to turn you in. I've had some pretty terrible adventures myself recently, and it's better for me to live under the Governor's protection. Besides, I'm also genuinely fond of his daughter. But that's all."

Briefly he told Mern about his recent adventures, and the zoologist listened to him attentively.

"For the time being," concluded Lien, "I've abandoned any hopes of directly incriminating Security on this F Station business, but I haven't changed my mind. I'm just looking for another angle. I've had the feeling that the Redfurs are another of the Company's embarrassing secrets, and maybe through them, I can get back at Security. I've read a lot of books lately on the subject, but they're all pretty obscure. Before Lukas, I read Tiaras' genetic study. It was hard to follow, especially for someone like me who doesn't know much about biology, but still interesting. I find certain of his hypothesis very troubling..."

Mern stopped to light up another nib, and looked around carefully to see if they were alone.

"You understand that I have to be very careful. Can you name another of the books that you've read; just to be sure."

"*Libzynski. Superstitions and Beliefs.* There's a chapter in it that deals with primitive religions, including the Ice People's. Dacan also devotes a chapter to the rapid growth of Redfur children; like animals, they can walk and run after only a couple of weeks...."

"That's enough, you've convinced me," Mern said, relieved. "You really are well versed on the subject. My original lecture at Merkur Station was going to be based on the works you just mentioned."

"I remember hearing at the time that you'd studied their basal metabolism. Something about the thyroid gland and enzymes, wasn't it?"

"Yes, but we shouldn't continue this conversation right now. Besides, I'm not crazy about this place," he said, looking at their surroundings.

"Where are you staying?"

"At the Terminus Hotel at the Company's expense. I guess I shouldn't complain too much. I have a good salary, but it's the endless travelling that's so exhausting. Also, it prevents me from doing any serious research... You mentioned Libzynski. I think his is one of the most interesting works..."

"The chapter he devoted to the Ice People seemed a bit brief to me," Lien said, not wholly convinced.

Mern stopped once more to light up a nib. He seemed to have difficulty breathing; too many of those cigars, was Lien's guess. Doctors advised against smoking more than a handful a day and special authorization was required to buy them. The Company wasn't against drug use per se, but liked to know who used them, and how much. If Mern continued his current usage, he would soon lose his sinecure and find himself demoted to some menial, bureaucratic position.

"Mmm. Yes. But Libzynski was rumored to have written many more notes on the subject, which weren't found among his papers after he died. I was once told by one of his assistants, that they contained a great deal of unpublished data about the Redfurs' myths, including a mention of some kind of deity called the Red Wolf."

Lien was disappointed.

"Well, wouldn't you think it normal for primitive people who have constant contact with deadly wolves to incorporate the species into their myths?"

"I'm not sure that's what Libzynski said. Unfortunately, I was only able to obtain fragments of his unpublished papers. From those I gather he was onto another kind of explanation altogether. Very different from what one would expect. But..."

Suddenly, he inhaled in fear. A Security patrol appeared, but passed the two men without even glancing their way.

"So it would be worthwhile to try to look for the rest of those notes?" Lien asked.

"Absolutely. I have some leads in my files. Odd references, trails I followed. I'll try to gather everything into something useable and give it to you. But I'm leaving tomorrow, and I don't want to meet you at the Governor's palace."

"I could come to your hotel," Lien suggested. "Say, tomorrow morning?"

"Well, why don't we have lunch, then?" the little man suggested shyly. "The restaurant is always empty at that time. About noon?"

"Noon it is," Lien said. He wondered briefly how he would explain his need to go out to Floa. But then he realized that after tonight's party, she would probably get up very late.

"Well, now that I'm here, I might as well walk you to the hotel," he offered.

"To continue with the matter of the Redfurs' thyroid gland, analysis showed that it was subjected to massive changes. Yet, one cannot say that they're idiots in the clinical sense of the term, as you would expect under these conditions. However, it is quite possible that they are not fully in possession of all their biological, nervous and mental faculties."

"Were you able to perform any analyses yourself?"

"Strangely enough, I was once able to perform an autopsy on the cadaver of a young Redfur that had been attacked and killed by wolves. I started examining some of the organs, but there was a Security mole on my team. Two days later, they came and removed the body. At the

143

time, they blamed it on rabies, which they said the Red-furs were carrying. And since the one I was studying had been bitten by wolves, it could have been true. At the time, I hadn't yet realized that there was such an absolute prohibition concerning the study of the Ice People. Absolute yet unofficial, since there are no laws against it. It's just that any research in that direction is strongly discouraged. I suspect that's why anthropology is no longer taught at the University."

They had reached the Hotel Terminus, a rather old and vast conglomeration of railcars parked in front of a dusty platform. It was a dump, and Lien found himself furious at the thought that a scientist of Hal Mern's caliber was relegated to such a fate.

When he returned to the party, Floa rushed towards him.

"Where were you? I looked all over for you."

"I went out for a while," he answered, without being more specific.

"I want to dance with you," she said, almost dragging him onto the dance floor.

From the way she ground her pelvis against his, he guessed that she had been excited by all the men who had probably been doing the same to her throughout the evening.

"We have to stay for at least another couple of hours," she sighed. "I don't want to. I want to be alone with you."

She whispered into his ear the things she wanted to do to him, and what she expected him to do in return. Her promises of erotic delights excited him, but he didn't forget his appointment with Hal Mern the next day. It was best for Floa to go to bed as late as possible.

"I don't think it'd be polite to go. We should stay."

144

"I don't know if I'll be able to," she pouted. "You always have such a good imagination; can't you come up with a good excuse for leaving?"

"No," he said firmly. "It would be very rude."

She got annoyed at him and refused to dance with him anymore. Worse, she flaunted herself in front of the other men for the rest of the evening, and flirted outrageously. Lien paid no attention and went back to the bar, where he joined a group talking about wolf hunts.

Suddenly, something caught his attention. It was Lieutenant Skoll, from Grand Star Station. He was standing at the other end of the room, looking in Lien's direction. The Glaciologist was deeply bothered by this, and emptied his glass. After he got a refill, he decided to be brave and check if the Lieutenant was indeed among the guests. But though he crossed the room several times and even looked in the bathrooms and the kitchens, he could find no trace of the Security man.

Why had the Lieutenant been invited to this party, if indeed he had? What was he doing in River Station? Was the Governor even aware of his presence in town?

It took all of Floa's amorous fervor to take his mind off those questions. In the loco-car on their return home, she embraced him with such abandon that he had to ask her to show some reserve, considering that the driver could see everything that went on in the cabin.

As soon as they had reached their private apartment, however, she took off her clothes and almost tore his off. She was always true to her word.

CHAPTER THIRTEEN

By taking careful precautions, Lien was able to slip out of their apartment by eleven o'clock. He went down to the kitchen for a cup of tea and hurried to leave the palace before Floa awoke. He took the Gregor Lukas book that Mern so wanted to read with him, hoping the little scientist would be able to make a photocopy of it and return it, since he hadn't yet finished it himself.

But there was an unpleasant surprise waiting for him at the Hotel Terminus; the desk clerk told him that Mern had been called back to Grand Star Station on an emergency, and had had to take the seven a.m. express.

"There were some problems at the zoo. Some of the animals got sick and they needed him in a hurry."

"When will he be back?"

"I don't have any idea. He didn't ask me to keep his room."

Lien went into a bar to have a vodka-laced tea and to think about the situation. Naively, it hadn't occurred to him that his long meeting with Mern the night before might have been witnessed and reported to Security. The consequences might be sinister for the poor zoologist, although they wouldn't dare attack him, since he was soon going to be the Governor's son-in-law.

Then, he remembered that he had briefly spotted Lieutenant Skoll. If Skoll had indeed been there, he might have had some connection with Mern's precipitate departure.

He thought regretfully about the precious fragments of Libzynski's notes that Mern was to have given him. Although, he suspected that these were probably on file somewhere within the Palace's library, and, with some patience, he would be able to find them. The Governor's library contained most of the books published since the beginning of the ice age, which, in fact, weren't that many, since most people had better things to do than write books. Also, real paper was a severely rationed commodity, because any timber that was dug up from under the ice was used for fuel rather than the manufacture of paper. His thoughts wandered to the sub-glacial Forest of Ots, and for a minute, he sadly remembered his friend Farrell, although the connection between the two escaped him.

Having nothing better to do, he went back to the Palace and locked himself in the library to look for more documents. He had only been there for a few minutes when the telephone rang. It was the receptionist.

"A long-distance call," she announced.

He immediately identified Mern's raucous and hard-breathing voice at the other end of the line.

"Don't ask me for explanations. Try looking in the New Encyclopedia, under Religions, for the information you want. You can go on by yourself from there. I don't have any more time. I've got to go. Good-bye."

The line went dead. Lien was still lost in his thoughts when Floa entered the room. She looked tired, and there were bags under her eyes.

"When did you get up? I didn't hear you. And you just couldn't wait to get back to this library, could you?"

"I didn't want to wake you, so..."

"That was really a dull party last night. But we had some real fireworks afterwards, didn't we, you wolf!"

Briefly, and rather inappropriately, he thought of the Red Wolf myth that Mern had mentioned. Floa saw that his attention was occupied somewhere else, and didn't force things.

"Well, I'm going to go back to bed."

"Okay. See you later."

As soon as she was gone, he went straight to the series of volumes that made up the New Encyclopedia, quickly locating the one that discussed Religions. At first, he was disappointed by the few lines devoted to the Ice People, but as soon as he read them he realized that they were powerfully important. They quoted Libzynski's work and mentioned the Redfurs' myth about the Red Wolf. Then, he spotted a footnote citing a later addition in a three-year old update.

But he was unable to find the update on the shelves. He thought it must have been filed under a different code, and that only further study of the catalog would enable him to find it. He decided to ask the librarian, but when he didn't seem to know either, Lien preferred not to be too specific. The mere mention of Libzynski's name might trigger some unpleasant consequences.

At dinner, the Governor announced that Lieutenant Skoll had been appointed head of Security for the Seventeenth District.

"I couldn't veto his appointment," the Governor added with barely contained anger, "but that man is dangerous. The Company is well aware that they're personally offending me by putting him here against my will, and I'm not through with this thing yet! Meanwhile, be careful, especially you, Lien. He's probably been sent here to keep a closer eye on you."

For the next three days, Lien looked for the Encyclopedia update. The library had boxes and boxes of unopened material. Lien took the opportunity to go through them and catalog them, for which the Librarian, who hadn't had the time to do it, was eternally grateful.

"I'm three years behind," he sighed. "When I got here, it was such a mess you wouldn't believe it, and I had other duties. I could only work two days a week."

The evening of the third day, Floa erupted in a fit of anger.

"Tonight, I want to go out! Go to a show, to a restaurant, anywhere but stay here and watch you read books!"

Lien sighed, because he was almost finished with his work, and he suspected that the update was in one of the few remaining unopened boxes, but he could hardly disagree with Floa.

"You're right. Where do you want to go," he said.

"A new cabaret just came into town; I've been told they have a good show. Naked girls, music, dancing, even magicians. It's called Cabaret Mikki."

Yeuse! The dancing girl that Farrell had met at Grand Star Station had worked for Cabaret Mikki. They were supposed to have gone to the Forest of Ots afterwards. That's why he had unconsciously associated the name of his late friend to the Forest. Hoping to see the girl again, he agreed with Floa's suggestion.

The show was more sophisticated than he would have thought. The naked girls didn't just exhibit themselves, but danced and sang rather well. Some of them also performed extremely elaborate numbers; Yeuse, in particular, was excellent in a strip-tease number based on the character of Marilyn Monroe.

Floa, who was never indifferent to any kind of erotic spectacle, commented in Lien's ear that she thought the girl was particularly attractive.

Later, Yeuse reappeared without the blonde wig that she had been wearing in the earlier number, and sang a series of funny ballads.

"Why don't we invite her to have a drink with us," Floa suggested. "Wouldn't you like to get acquainted with her?"

Lien, who was well aware that Floa was not adverse to an erotic interlude with other members of her sex, answered without jealousy.

"Don't put it like that. You're the one who wants to get better acquainted!"

Floa smiled, and summoned the maitre d'. Later, Yeuse came over to their table. She was dressed in a floor-length white gown, which at first looked rather demure and out of place, until one noticed that it was slit all the way up to her shoulders on either side.

"It's nice to see you again. Thank you for the invitation," she told Lien.

"What?" Floa said, "You two already know each other?"

"I heard about Farrell's death," Yeuse continued. "I'm glad to see that you weren't with him."

Lien felt awkward and didn't know how to answer. Her dark eyes were boring into his soul and he suddenly realized that she had never been very far from his thoughts since the first moment they met. His feeling that there was something missing and the fugitive impression of nostalgia and loneliness that he had experienced from time to time had really been thoughts of her. It dawned on him that he was in love with a woman whom he had only met once, briefly, in the corridor of his old train.

"I was the only survivor," he said, without volunteering any more details.

"You knew Farrell?" Floa said. "Now I understand why Lien didn't put up more of a fight about coming here tonight."

Suddenly, she started watching the two of them with calculating and suspicious eyes, trying to uncover some secret that might exist between them, or catch some confidence that might be about her. Lien knew that she could be enormously jealous, petty, and even cruel.

"You're the one who suggested we invite her over," he reminded her.

Yeuse turned towards Floa, her deep gaze almost seeming to undress the young woman, who blushed. Lien, who had never seen her blush before, was surprised.

"You're extremely beautiful," Yeuse said. "Why don't you two come to my dressing room? I still have one number to perform."

Her dressing room turned out to be a very small cabin with a narrow bunk for sleeping and a dressing table. The air smelled like Yeuse, not an artificial, perfumed smell, but the good and natural odor of her skin.

"Tell me more about Farrell's death," Yeuse said.

"No," Floa replied. "We shouldn't talk about it. It's an old story, and there's nothing we can do to change it. Besides, it's dangerous."

Yeuse took her hand and kissed it very gently. Floa shivered and her eyes betrayed her desire. Through the slits of the white dress, she could see Yeuse's statuesque body, full, firm and rounded. Involuntarily, she whetted her lips with several, quick darting movements of her tongue.

"Well, if that's what you really want," she said languidly.

Yeuse sat on the bunk next to Floa, who laid her head in the dancer's lap. While Lien began his story, Yeuse's fingers softly traced every feature of Floa's face, caressing her and exploring her mouth. The engineer had trouble concentrating on his narrative, so erotic was the picture of the two women. He began at the start of their ill-fated survey expedition and, without omitting any details, told her the full story of his adventures.

"When I was in the North, I heard a rumor about several of F Station's trains being either lost or sent to a concentration camp," Yeuse said.

"The truth is that all those people are now lying frozen at the bottom of an ice canyon."

Floa sighed with a mixture of pleasure from Yeuse gently toying with her ear, and fear at being forced to remember the horrible events.

"So you decided not to come forward with the truth," Yeuse said, without any hint of reproach.

"We were afraid."

"Yes," Floa whined. "I want to live. I want to be happy and forget those horrible things."

"Everyone says that Security is going to take over the Company soon. I've heard that they've been buying back shares from all the small stockholders; that if you're a small stockholder, you have endless problems with the Law until one day, a Security man appears and offers to buy your stock. Some people sell because they want to be left in peace. The ones who don't are sent to the Front, where they die. Their heirs are usually more flexible. Security is gathering it all, two shares here, four there. Soon, they'll have enough for a controlling interest, and then, they'll set up the kind of dictatorship they dream of..."

Floa took hold of Yeuse's long, perfectly manicured hand, and started kissing her fingers.

"I've also heard that Security is nothing but a front; that they're secretly being supported by the Neo-Catholic Church, which threatens the faithful with eternal damnation. They despise the idle, decadent executives who run this Company."

Floa had taken Yeuse's hand and put it on her left breast. The Governor's daughter seemed to be almost in a state of ecstasy, when suddenly the interphone crackled with the voice of the dwarf who acted as the show's stage manager.

"Closing number in two minutes! Closing number in two minutes!"

Yeuse stood up and went to her dressing table. She took off her gown and hung it carefully. She had been naked beneath the flimsy fabric. Floa moaned softly, and fell to her knees in front of the girl, but Yeuse gently pushed her away.

"Not now. Later..." she said.

She helped Floa to lie back down on the bunk, and finished her preparations. This consisted of covering her pubic area with a large, cut-out red star, then sprinkling sequins over the rest of her body. Lien helped her do her back, and Floa, who was biting her lips, could see that he was aroused.

"I'll be back in fifteen minutes," Yeuse said, before walking out.

They remained alone. Instead of the jealousy he had expected, Lien could read another, even stronger emotion in Floa's eyes. This too was jealousy, but of another kind. Floa would have killed him to keep Yeuse to herself.

"Go away. Leave us alone," Floa finally said.

He remained there, silent and unmoving.

"Go away," she said, almost choking. "When I invited her, I didn't know, I didn't suspect I'd feel this way. I thought we would have a threesome, but now I can't stand the thought of sharing her with you. I don't want you to be there."

"I want her too," Lien said very softly.

"She's more than a lover. I don't know if you can understand. She's almost like a... mother."

Lien said nothing.

"Please, go away before she comes back," Floa begged. "With any other girl, we could have been together, but not her. For me, please?"

Lien nodded and left. He checked out his coat and decided to walk back to the palace. He needed the walk, and the feeling of the cold night air with its smell of ozone and sulphur to calm his desire.

When he arrived at the palace, he remembered the Encyclopedia update and, since he had a key to the library, he decided to continue his search. Eventually, he located it in the last box. The article on Libzynski was more important than he had dreamed. Lien learned that it was because of this historian, a specialist in religions, that the Neo-Catholics had been able to rediscover all the dogma of the ancient Catholic Church. This was news to Lien. He continued looking for any mention of the Ice People, until he came across a significant passage:

"For several years, Libzynski tried to spend at least several weeks amongst the different, primitive tribes of Ice People, in order to gather new information about their culture and religion...

"After four years of research, he was finally able to confirm that the Redfurs were basically monotheistic. Their primary god was known as the Red Wolf, who had created the Ice People, but who was also responsible for their perpetual travels upon the ice. There were a number of related myths surrounding the Red Wolf, such as his creation of both Salt and Sugar, two substances which play an important role in the Redfurs' lives...

"Towards the end of his life, Libzynski postulated a new theory so strange and controversial that it cannot in all legitimacy be reproduced here. Now that the controversy has died down, it would be unseemly to revive it. For more information, however, researchers would profit by looking at the notes left by Libzynski, which are kept at the Fiona Station library, his last residence. It was there where he had felt he was certain to eventually locate the final proof of his incredible theories."

Lien felt like screaming with frustration. Not a word about Libzynski's so-called controversial theories. He felt as if Hal Mern had sent him on a wild goose chase.

Then, he reread the article and realized that he had actually been given a significant clue. Fiona Station. Why had Libzynski believed he could find the proof of his theories on the origin of the Redfurs there? Lien thought for a few seconds, then looked for another book that listed all the stations, including name changes that had occurred during the previous centuries. He had never heard of Fiona Station, but intended to find out what had happened to it. When he did, it was almost anti-climactic. Its name had been changed years before to F Station.

CHAPTER FOURTEEN

When he woke up, Lien was surprised to see that Floa was not lying next to him; disappointed, he thought she had probably spent the night with Yeuse. But when he looked in the neighboring bedroom, he noticed that she was there, sleeping peacefully. Obviously, she had come back late and had not wanted to wake him up. He couldn't help but wonder, however, if that encounter with Yeuse was not going to have a deep affect on their relationship.

At ten o'clock he was back at Cabaret Mikki, which, exceptionally, had been parked in the center of town. Normally, travelling shows were expected to park along the periphery.

The dwarf was sitting on the metal steps of one of the Cabaret's rail cars, smoking a cigar; Lien asked if he could see Yeuse.

"She's out. I think she went shopping, or to get a haircut..."

Without much hope at first, he followed the directions the dwarf had given him. But his perseverance was soon rewarded, when he saw her coming towards him. She smiled and kissed him tenderly on the cheek.

"Let's have a drink," she suggested.

He took her to a plush bar that had been decorated to look like a Spanish patio, complete with torrid heat, potted greens and flamenco music.

"Did you ever wonder why we spend so much time copying our ancestors?" she asked, commenting upon the decor. "It's as if our civilization can't produce anything new. But then again, we barely manage to survive. Even in love we exhibit the same vices and perversions.

156

That girlfriend of yours, Floa, wanted to make love to me last night. I didn't want to. She was really unhappy about it."

Lien, on the other hand, was happy to find out that nothing had happened between the two women.

"I suppose there's always the Redfurs, but that's frowned upon."

Automatically, he looked up, but being inside, he couldn't see the dome.

"I thought about you a lot," he said.

"Me too, but that was only because you were Farrell's friend. He was a very nice man. I'm not the promiscuous type, and I don't go to bed with everyone who asks me, but your friend was extremely persuasive. Besides, I was feeling lonely that night..."

They were silent, then, she continued.

"Are you going to marry her?"

They both knew she meant Floa.

"I don't know," he replied candidly.

"You need her father's protection."

"Now more than ever," he admitted.

The waiter brought them two glasses of xeres, a warm, sweet Spanish wine. It wasn't the real thing, of course, but no one was able to tell the difference.

"You're continuing with your research?"

"Last night I made an incredible discovery."

"That's right; you went home while I was doing the closing number. Floa refused to tell me why you'd left. What happened?"

"She begged me to leave."

"I guess at first, you'd planned to have a threesome with me, hadn't you?"

He nodded silently. Yeuse closed her eyes and he understood that he had hurt her feelings.

"You think an exotic dancer is no more than a whore, don't you? You wanted me, both of you. Would you have asked her to leave? Why didn't you stay?"

"I didn't dare."

"Was it a test? I slept with your best friend, so you wanted to see if I would do it with your girl friend too?"

"No, it wasn't like that. Believe me."

She smiled, and he could see that she no longer felt bitter.

"So you went home and made a discovery?"

"Yes, but it's complicated to explain. Have you heard about Libzynski?"

"No. Who is he?"

"Was. He lived about fifty years ago and died in a place named Fiona Station."

He then explained to her who Libzynski was, and why he was interested in his work.

"I've never heard of that place," she said.

"Its name was later changed to F Station. Apparently, Libzynski went there because he felt he could find some evidence to substantiate whatever theories he had about the Ice People's Red Wolf myth. I think at least part of the reason the Company got rid of it was to bury all traces of Libzynski's theories. Literally, as it turned out. The rebellion was just a cover story."

Yeuse looked at Lien with a mixture of wonder and suspicion.

"I'm not crazy," he vehemently argued. "I'm not making this all up just to pursue some kind of personal revenge. These are facts."

"Maybe it's just a coincidence."

"Maybe. But a coincidence of this magnitude sure looks like design to me. F Station turns out to be Fiona Station, where Libzynski spent the last years of his life trying to prove a theory that was so controversial that, today no one will even acknowledge its existence. Then, there's a resurgence of interest in the subject, by Hal Mern and maybe others like him. F Station is convicted of rebellion and its population is sent to its death in an icy pit. And now it's my turn to look for clues, to try to piece the whole mystery together. I have the feeling that the two thousand corpses I saw there will turn out to be just a statistic, and a small one at that, in a secret story that covers centuries of oppression."

Later, Lien would, for the first, time wonder about the shrouded beginnings of the ice age. The survivors had turned to the rail companies to provide a vital link between communities isolated by vast icy wastelands. Rail could carry power at a time when all other forms of transportation had become impossible, and power was life. Soon, the Companies grew, spinning their metal web all across the planet, constantly laying new layers of rails so that, in some places, they covered hundreds of miles. But still it wasn't enough. Under the guidance of the C.A.N.Y.S.T., it was decided that immobility in this new ice age was not only dangerous but illegal. First, the buildings themselves, such as hospitals, cabarets, barracks, etc. had been put on wheels. Then, it was the turn of entire cities, which in the process were rechristened Stations. The old world was erased, and a new one was told to keep moving. Thanks to the rails, the Companies provided power, food, entertainment, culture and every amenity that was needed for life in the ice age. People no longer were "citizens" or "comrades" but "Voyagers", a new label reflecting their status as eternal travelers. They were effectively uprooted from any semblance of social continuity, while they became dependent on the Companies for all aspects of their lives. The Companies needed

159

only to threaten to turn off the power to quell any attempt at revolt. The cold itself would take care of the rest. Or, they could suddenly decide to move an entire town, or village, from one place to another; there would be little violence, almost no blood. One day, a Station would simply disappear, and no one would know what had happened to its inhabitants. They would have disappeared forever into the white shroud of the ice.

"So what do you think happened to Libzynski?" she asked.

"Obviously he'd made some important discovery about the origin of the Redfurs. There has to be something more behind this story of the Red Wolf, than simply being the symbol of creation. Libzynski looked for it in F Station until his death, and I have to do the same. I'm going back to that canyon to look and look until I find what it is."

"You're probably crazy, but I think I understand."

She took his hand in hers and kept it there.

"How are you going to do it?"

"I don't know yet. I need some breathing space. If I leave Floa, I'm sure Lieutenant Skoll will arrest me, and this time, they'll get rid of me forever."

"I'll help you. I don't know how, but I'll find a way."

"I'll look for some more information in the library, and then I'll make plans to go back there."

Driven by some kind of inner demon, he had completely forgotten that he had sworn to himself that he would never go back to the dead, or their secrets, which waited for him at the bottom of the huge canyon in the Bia Sector.

CHAPTER FIFTEEN

The loco-car was nearing the Bia Sector when Floa called Lien on the radio. Her voice seemed somehow altered by the loudspeaker, but in truth, it was her own rage which distorted it.

"Lien, you come back here right now or I'll tell Security that you've stolen my loco-car; you have until tonight to get back to River Station. Is that slut Yeuse with you?"

The Glaciologist switched off the radio and looked at the beautiful, dark-haired dancer.

"If she does it, Security will have a field day. My last and only protection turning against me!"

Later, she insisted on going outside with him.

"We've got to be careful about the wolves. Now that the Redfurs are gone, they might have come back."

"You know, I read once that they were almost extinct, but the Companies brought them back through a secret breeding program. They wanted the outside to continue to have the image of being a vast territory totally hostile to man, so that we would be more willing to stay penned up in our trains."

They put on their isothermal suits and carefully stepped out. After following the rail line for a few yards, Lien suddenly grabbed his companion's arm. There, in front of them, was no longer a chasm, but a vast pile of crumbled ice rocks.

"The canyon! It's gone!"

He looked around to make sure that it wasn't his senses which had betrayed him. He even dropped to his hands and knees in a fruitless effort to remove some of the smaller blocks to at least find some traces of the former crevice. It was useless; the wrecks and their victims now lay buried under tons of ice.

"It was here, Yeuse," he said. "It was here."

She helped him to stand. For more than an hour he examined every inch of the land, hoping to find something they may have forgotten, but it all looked so different that he couldn't even be sure that this was the same place. Eventually, they decided to return to the loco-car; Lien moved like an automaton.

"They tried to erase whatever remained of Libzynski here," Yeuse said, "but what about the rest of F Station? That's still somewhere in the North. Why don't we try to find it?"

Lien smiled weakly. He understood that Yeuse was trying to offer him a ray of hope, to turn his thoughts from disappointment towards a remote possibility of success.

"I guess we can try," he said. "We have this loco-car with its black box. We can go anywhere, at least as long as Floa doesn't go to Security. But how can we stop her?"

Yeuse paled.

"I think I can do it," she said. "I know her price. Drop me off at Cross Station and keep going North. I'll go back to River Station and see Floa. I can always catch up with you later."

"I can't let you do it, Yeuse. I can't!"

"Why? Does it really matter? I don't think so. Besides, it's my decision, not yours."

When they got back inside the loco-car, she went directly to the radio and called Floa. When the Governor's daughter realized it was Yeuse calling, her voice completely changed, becoming soft and sweet. She didn't even mention Security.

"I'll be waiting for you," she finally said.

"She'll be furious when she sees you're alone," Lien said after the communication had been broken. "And even more furious when she finds out that I'm travelling North in her loco-car."

"I'll take her mind off it," Yeuse said, smiling.

She was impressed by their rapid progress; the black box enabled them to pass not only freight trains and regular passenger trains, but military and troop convoys. They reached Cross Station in record time.

Lien felt guilty as he left Yeuse on the platform in the middle of all the livestock traders, who had never looked so loutish before. Soon afterwards, he was speeding along towards the Great North. Eventually, he would have to refuel, but he hadn't wanted to do it at Cross Station where he had been accused of black marketeering. The Official Railway Guide told him the location of the nearest refueling station; he radioed them in advance and gave them his clearance number. However, they answered very politely that they were just out of fuel because a huge military convoy had depleted all their stock.

At first, he didn't give it a second thought and kept driving; although he slowed down to conserve fuel so that he would be able to reach the next refueling station. When he received a similar answer there, he understood that Security was trying to prevent him from going North.

"But I have absolute priority," he insisted.

"So? You could be the Governor himself and I couldn't give you any fuel if I didn't have any," the attendant said rather rudely.

Hastily he looked for the nearest town. As luck would have it, it was Ots Station, the town located in the sub-glacial forest.

The rail tracks entered a huge ice tunnel that grew larger and larger. Soon, the view was staggering. The tracks snaked between huge trees, perfectly fossilized in the sub-glacial caverns; some, like firs, pines, larches, and oaks, still had all their leaves. There were trees as far as the eye could see. The loco-car's headlights made the ice glisten for miles ahead. Convoys of timber continually appeared from the other direction.

He had visited Ots Station once before and had not forgotten this town, whose entire reason for being was the timber business. Because of that, it had a special character. The sidings were filled with saloons, cabarets and gambling halls. The miners were paid huge salaries, which they spent as fast as they could take it from their pockets. There were hundreds of prostitutes, living in cars as diverse as a super-Pullman to an old drafty box-car. Ots was also one of the very rare, domeless cities. It had been dug inside the ice itself and, as a result, the air was noticeably colder than in other cities.

They refused him service at the refueling station in spite of his priority clearance.

"Impossible," said the agent. "We just received override instructions freezing our stocks. Apparently, there's going to be a major offensive on the Front, and the Army'll need additional fuel reserves."

Lien knew it was useless to insist, so instead, he went around the bars and cafes, offering large sums of money for fuel vouchers. After several hours he'd been moderately successful, although he was still far from his objective. Then, two suspicious-looking men offered to supply him with the balance of what he needed.

"Meet us at Platform 85 in a half-hour," one said. "We'll wait for you."

As Lien started to leave, a young man near the bar signaled him discreetly. Lien went over to him.

"Don't do it, Voyager," the boy said. "I know those guys. They're crooks. They'll kill you and steal your loco-car."

"But I need fuel," Lien said, "at any price."

"Why don't you just use electric power like everyone else?"

"I have a black box, but if I use the Company's power, that'll slow me down because I won't be able to pass all the other trains. It'll just cause trouble."

"Why don't you try Gaha, on Platform 19. I'll go with you, she knows me."

Lien took the young man back to his loco-car. Once inside he whistled in amazement; it was probably the first time in his life that he had seen anything that luxurious.

"Can you take me with you when you leave?" he asked. "I was exempted from military service because of my bad eyes, and they sent me here to mine trees instead. I want to go join up with a bunch of friends who are Outsiders, and live on a commune in the North. They're completely self-sufficient. They raise reindeer and use the methane from the dung to make their own power. Things are really working out okay for them."

"Okay, if you can get me some fuel," Lien said.

Gaha was an enormously fat woman who ran an obviously thriving black market operation. Eventually, she and Lien reached an agreement and money changed hands. Soon, the loco-car's tank was full, and they were able to leave Ots Station; Lien adjusted the speed to get the best mileage out of the engine. His newly-acquired friend was extremely talkative, and soon the Glaciologist learned more about Ots than he'd ever dreamed possible. He discovered that there were rebel miners hiding in rogue galleries dug in as yet unexplored parts of the forest. They were criminals, and deserters from the Front, and sometimes they launched attacks against the Station, looting food and supplies.

"Sometimes, I can tell you, there are really bloody fights. That's when it's better to get out of the way and let Security handle it."

Eventually, they reached Baltic Station, which was a major Northern junction. Lien's companion asked to be dropped off there. Lien gave him some money to help him with the rest of his trip.

"I'm here to find out where they sent F Station," the Glaciologist explained as they were shaking hands.

"Now that you mention it, I seem to remember having heard that it had been sent to the Front to help dig tunnels," the other replied before they separated.

Lien wasted a several hours before he found a clerk who was willing to give him some information.

"They wouldn't allow it inside Baltic Station," the man said, "all the tracks would've been jammed. They split it into separate convoys, which were still pretty big; the smallest one took up a full twenty rails. I think they sent it to the Polar Network. Some friends of mine told me they'd found traces, you know, garbage, stuff like that..."

"Thanks for your help," Lien said, then tried to give the man some money, which he refused.

"I'm against deporting whole cities like that. I guess you're trying to find someone from the town?"

Lien nodded without being more specific.

"Then be careful. The Polar Network is under constant surveillance. The Siberians managed to short-circuit it once and all the trains were paralyzed for a week."

"It's almost at the Front then?"

"It is the Front. You could get blown up by a mine, or a missile up there. Just yesterday a passenger train was destroyed just like that."

Undaunted by the man's story, Lien switched onto the Polar Network. Only a few miles away from Baltic Station he began seeing signs of fighting, and realized he had entered a frightening new world. His loco-car had never seemed as small as it did then, travelling between huge metal monsters covered with cannons and missile-launchers. Once, he saw a three thousand foot long destroyer, with superstructures six hundred feet above ground. It needed fifty tracks to move, and was shooting a barrage of flame and steel at the enemy lines somewhere on the other side of the ice cliffs. The noise of its cannons, and the vibrations caused by its slow movement, turned the entire area into a hellish place of pandemonium and terror. From the driver's seat, Lien could see the rails undulate on the ice, but thanks to his black box, he was still receiving priority passage, the same as the small loco-cars that were used as mobile command posts by the military chiefs.

He also saw hospital trains leaving the Front. They were almost endlessly long and had no priority at all. They looked decrepit, and their crematoriums spilled oily, black clouds from the back.

Suddenly, he found himself in the paradoxical position of being stuck in a local traffic jam caused by other vehicles also equipped with black boxes. His speed dramatically decreased to no more than that of a man on foot. Finally, he was forced to stop. He could see a group of generals and colonels arguing; drivers were frantically running around as they tried to discover what was going on. There had obviously been an accident but, eventually, the line was cleared and all the cars continued on their way. Lien had programmed his to remain on the Polar Network, and was looking for an opportunity to stop and inquire about F Station.

At one point, he was almost stopped at a Security checkpoint. Isolated vehicles were dispatched towards a parking line where the identity of their passengers was carefully checked. Thanks to his black box, Lien was able to bypass it; but, he didn't know for how long he would be able to do so.

Tired and hungry, he eventually decided to stop at a small military outpost called Meridian Station. He found a restaurant catering to soldiers on leave and a thriving local prostitution racket. Meridian Station was obviously a makeshift leave town set up by, and for, the military. He made careful inquiries about F Station and getting more fuel. Eventually, a fat Sergeant offered to sell him some jerry cans. Lien followed him to a warehouse where the transaction would be completed. As the officer was emptying the contents of the cans into the tank of Lien's railcar, the Glaciologist again asked about F Station.

"Why do you want to go there?" the man asked suspiciously. "No one ever goes there."

"Secret mission," Lien replied curtly. "As you can see, I have a black box."

"Understood," the Sergeant said, visibly impressed. "But it's incredibly dangerous. F Station is parked on a line in a no man's land right between our fire and that of the Siberians. It's gotta be hell there."

"A single line? I thought it needed at least a dozen tracks to move."

"It did, but they broke it up more into a single, long convoy that they put on the Arctic Circle Line."

Once he was again alone, Lien looked at Floa's Guide. The Arctic Circle Line was basically what its name implied, a line that more or less followed the ancient Arctic Circle. And it was headed straight towards the Front, just like the Sergeant had said.

To get there, he had to travel through another junction called Kola Station, full of military convoys, many with priorities equal to his.

As he neared it, he was suddenly switched to a secondary line. At first, he wasn't concerned about it, and, conceitedly, even thought that his black box was using its priority signals to find a way to detour the town. But it didn't take long for him to realize that such was not the case. An outside force had overridden his box, and his car was now being remotely piloted from elsewhere.

Eventually, the loco-car slowed to a standstill in front of a Security checkpoint. Three guards came on board to check his papers.

"I'm on a mission for the Company," he tried to bluff.

The Security officer was polite, but observed that his black box contained no instructions regarding his mission.

"I expect to receive further instructions at Kola Station," Lien said, trying to save the situation.

"No problem; in that case, I'm sure you won't see any objection to us accompanying you, Voyager. We can't ever be too careful."

He was then taken in tow by a Security patrol car, which kept its gun pointed at him throughout the short journey.

Then, still under vigilant escort, Lien was taken to the Security Headquarters of Kola Station. In his head, he rehearsed various escape scenarios, even if it meant abandoning the loco-car. He could always find another way to reach F Station now that he knew where it was.

"Take him to Room 7," the receptionist said. "They've been waiting for him."

This struck Lien as very ominous indeed. If they had been waiting for him, it meant that his chances of escape were nonexistent. Security had obviously allowed him to get to Kola Station, at the center of the Front, and decided to stop his odyssey here.

"I knew we would meet again," Lieutenant Skoll said as Lien entered the room.

CHAPTER SIXTEEN

Skoll ordered the Security guards to leave, and asked Lien to sit down.

"How did you get here?" the Glaciologist asked.

"I took the direct route."

"But how did you know that I would make it to Kola Station? I couldn't get fuel during most of my trip."

"I know. I'm the one who gave the orders. I didn't really have a choice, you understand, but I had complete faith in your resourcefulness."

Lien was confused. Skoll seemed to be saying that he had wanted him to make it to Kola Station, but not officially.

"You've been very active lately, Lien Rag, and I've been very interested in your activities. I take it you were looking for F Station? Did you really believe you could get there by yourself?"

"Sure; I almost made it, and I still might."

"Indeed, and I'm going to help you."

He pulled out a nib and lit it while Lien was still trying to figure out the Lieutenant's motivations.

"You've been a constant headache for both the Company and Security from the beginning of all this. Since we started acquiring Company stock from the minority shareholders, Sadon and his daughter have been trying to find some kind of information they could use against us in order to maintain their secure power base. They heard about F Station, and knew something was going on in the Bia Sector, so they pulled strings to send you there, hoping that you would bring back some kind of evidence to prove Security wrongdoing. It turned out that you did, but we were able to arrange a convincing cover-up, and turn the situation to our advantage. In fact, we were so successful that we managed to completely scare the Governor and his daughter off our tails. We thought you'd follow the same course, but surprisingly, you didn't. Instead, you displayed an amazing sense of investigative ability by uncovering some of the layers of truth we'd fabricated, and by turning your attention to the matter of the Ice People..."

Lien was paying careful attention to Skoll's speech. Normally, the Lieutenant should have had him arrested immediately and either executed or dumped in a camp. Why was he talking freely with him instead and saying he would help him to reach F Station?

"As soon as I saw you with Hal Mern at that party, I knew that you'd stumbled onto something. I gave orders to have him recalled, but it was too late. He'd had the time to provide you with the missing piece of information you needed to connect Libzynski to F Station..."

Lien could not hide his surprise. Skoll smiled.

"Oh, yes, I'm quite familiar with the works of Lukas, Dacan, and Libzynski. You were absolutely correct in assuming that all the manuscripts he left to the town library are now, unfortunately, at the bottom of the Bia canyon, buried under tons of ice. You were also right in surmising that there might still be copies in other parts of F Station; we'll go to look for them together."

"Why do you care about any of this? And, frankly, I'm not sure that I trust you. You do work for Security."

Skoll once again smiled mysteriously, and raised a finger into the air.

"Come with me," he said. "We can't talk about this here. It's too dangerous."

Puzzled, Lien watched as he walked towards the door and invited him to follow; they walked out together. The Guards were gone and the Lieutenant took him back to Floa's loco-car.

Once inside, Skoll took off his jacket and a sweater he wore underneath. Lien was amazed to discover that the Lieutenant's body was covered by a layer of thick, reddish fur.

"When I go through a medical check, I'm careful to shave, but I'm always worried about being found out..."

Seeing Lien's stupefaction, he added.

"Yes, I'm a half-breed. My mother was a poor, Ia-kut woman, without much civilized culture. She still lived in primitive conditions in the Northernmost Districts, probably very much like her ancestors must have. One day, she met a tribe of Ice People and became pregnant by one of them. Later, she moved to a domed town, where she lived as a servant, and she took me with her. At the time, I didn't have any fur, so I could pass for normal. It began to grow when I became a teen-ager, except on my face, hands and feet. A lucky genetic accident, I guess. But I always knew that my father was one of those primitives living out there, somewhere. I only feel sadness and shame when I see them toiling on our domes and eating our refuse. That's why I've always been secretly interested in the origins of my father's race."

"So the merciless, intransigent Security Lieutenant was just a front?"

"Not completely. I despise the decadent executives who think of themselves as civilized; when I can find legal ways of making them suffer, I do. But we have work to do. Wait for me here."

Skoll left, and during his absence, Lien wondered if it wasn't just another elaborate trap to make him confess what he had discovered about Libzynski's work. But that didn't really make sense, since it was obvious that Skoll knew as much, if not more, than he did.

The Lieutenant returned two hours later. If he really was a half-breed, Lien could understand why he felt driven to fathom the secrets of the Redfurs' origins.

"Let's go," he said.

He took a black metallic card, and inserted it into the black box.

"This will get us to F Station without any hassles. It's been cut off from the main network for a week, but we should be able to make it."

Lien saw the first shell explode about three hundred feet from the tracks and, for a few seconds, he felt as if he'd never left the Front. Then, they were in hell. But Skoll didn't seem to be paying any attention to what was happening outside. Two hundred feet away, a trainload of fuel exploded with a deafening barrage of sound. Lien saw a few men who had been turned into living torches try to run away or roll themselves against the ice, which was melting and congealing into a pool of oily reflections.

Further away, gigantic cranes resembling prehistoric monsters were busy clearing wrecks off the tracks. A fleet of high-speed destroyers rolled by; its blazing guns pierced the milky polar night.

"This skirmish has been going on for three days. We're trying to hold on to a crucial junction and it's difficult, because the ground is getting downright swampy. There are some hot water springs that are turning the ice into mush, and we need to constantly reinforce the tracks. They've even used pontoons in some places. But it's still the best passage; there are huge ice cliffs everywhere else."

They came across huge machines that were laying down new tracks at a rapid pace. They were almost entirely automatic, and didn't need many human operators. The rails were supported by prongs that dug deep down into the ice shelf. Once dug in, several hooks exploded at the other extremity to anchor the rail firmly. The line was then strong enough to support a ten thousand ton destroyer if need be.

Suddenly, less than two hundred feet away, the rails twisted under the impact of a missile, rising into the air like the tentacles of a flailing octopus and remaining stuck there like a nightmarish roller-coaster ride.

"We're stuck," Lien said, looking in the rearview monitor. "There's traffic behind us."

"They'll clear it fast," Skoll replied.

And indeed, the black box's priority signals worked their magic, forcing all the other vehicles to back up quickly and enable Lien's loco-car to reach a cross junction.

"But we're facing the wrong way!" Lien shouted.

"I know. But it won't matter."

They were now moving in reverse at an alarming speed on the wrong side of the track. But the black box continued to send signals diverting the traffic, or freezing it on sidings, so they could progress unhindered. Soon, they reached another junction, and Skoll's clever maneuvering got them back on the right line, this time facing in the right direction.

The enemy's bombardments continued. They passed a light cruiser lying overturned on the ice. It was burning, melting the ice beneath it and sinking into it at the same time. Soon it would be gone, swallowed whole by the ice.

"If it's one of the nuclear-powered models," Skoll remarked, "It'll eventually reach the surface of the planet, and maybe even sink below that."

"What about the radiation?" asked Lien, "Won't that be a problem?"

"Eventually the Company will clean it up. Meanwhile, it's more important to consolidate the Eastern Front against the Siberians. For the time being, the Pan-American has remained neutral, but what if they decide to ally themselves with the Siberians? That would mean war on two Fronts."

A huge dreadnought that took up fifteen tracks passed by, blasting a barrage of fiery death ahead of it. With each shot, over a hundred shells flew to bring death and destruction to the enemy. The spectacle was almost beautiful in its horror. The huge train was surrounded by red and green glows, and purple and yellow hazes, making an iris of color that contrasted startlingly with the dull, icy grayness of the surrounding world.

Not long after, they came across a number of bodies lying next to the line. Obviously, an armored train had exploded on a mine, and had split in two. The explosion had projected soldiers everywhere. Some wore their isothermal suits; others hadn't had the time to put them on. Most of them were already dead or dying, their bodies purple from the cold. Skoll didn't even slow down.

"Wait a minute," Lien said. "There may be injured men. I don't want a victory at that price."

"We can't take them all. They're doomed to die from the cold anyway; the hospital train won't be here for hours yet."

They didn't stop.

Further on, they saw a line of men walking along the tracks in the opposite direction, as if they were retreating; for the first time, Skoll appeared concerned.

"The line must be broken up ahead, otherwise they wouldn't be trying to rejoin the rear lines on foot..."

Ten miles later, they saw the biggest wreck they had ever seen. Hundreds of rail cars, cruisers, even destroyers, lay mangled across the landscape. Lien guessed that this had been the theatre of a recent confrontation.

They looked for a clear passage somewhere between the wrecks, zigzagging between tracks, taking junctions in reverse. Eventually, by a sheer stroke of luck, Skoll found a single track that had miraculously been preserved, lying between a missile launcher, and an armored fortress whose engine had been blown up. They took it carefully; progressing at a snail's pace, using their lasers to cut their way through projecting shards of metal.

When they reached the other side, they saw that it was blocked with Siberian trains, all as badly destroyed and mangled as the Trans-European forces. Lien could not even begin to guess at the number of men who were probably lying dead beneath this huge, metal graveyard.

"We're in Siberian territory now," Skoll said, "but I think they've pulled back some. We must have won that last battle, technically at least. There's still a risk of running into a patrol car or a lone cruiser, though. F Station was parked on a line that's coming up on our left. I hope the switches still work."

But when they reached them, they'd all been blocked. Lien offered to go out to try to fix one. He put on his isothermal suit and tried to unstick it with a mining bar, but couldn't.

Suddenly, Skoll joined him outside. He didn't wear any protective clothing, and didn't seem to suffer from the cold.

"Let me have a try."

With a show of strength that would have seemed incredible for normal people, he pushed on the switch and managed to force it open, causing the ice to splinter violently in all directions.

"Now, I do believe you," Lien said. "No one who's not part Redfur could have done what you just did."

Skoll smiled, but said nothing. They returned to the loco-car and drove for another twenty miles, until they reached a small, domeless station, made up of nothing but a few isothermal cars connected to each other.

"The line is broken up ahead; we'll have to do the rest on foot. It's about three miles. Can you do it? There's no other way."

"You mean F Station is three miles from here?"

"No, I mean its three miles until our next transportation."

Skoll had to walk more slowly than usual because of Lien, but the Glaciologist managed to keep pace. They followed the tracks until they turned into broken metal shards buried under ice blocks. Soon afterwards they saw a thin column of smoke. As they walked towards it, Lien saw a small man, all bundled up in furs, but wearing no isothermal suit. His face was protected with shiny, greasy layers of animal fat. Skoll addressed the man in a tongue that was unknown to Lien, but which he guessed to be Iakut.

The Iakut gestured that they were to follow him, and they reached a small village of a hunters in reindeer skins. Lien also noticed some sleds with fierce-looking dogs -- or maybe they were wolves? -- tied to them.

Skoll pulled some money out of his pocket and turned to Lien.

"Do you have any dollars?"

"Yes, but they're inside. I need to find a warm place to open my suit."

They took him inside a tent where a group of women and children sat around an ancient, foul smelling, furnace.

"Seal oil," explained Skoll. "We're on the Arctic ice shelf here. There are places where the ice isn't too thick, and they can still hunt seals like their ancestors used to do."

Soon afterwards, they left the Iakut campsite in a sled pulled by dogs. The Iakut had told Skoll that they might meet a couple of tribes of Ice People on the Shelf, but that they were on good terms with them.

They stopped for the night and, in spite of the protection of his suit, Lien didn't feel particularly secure, knowing that he was alone, a man of the warmth, in the middle of the arctic ice shelf. The dogs, who howled eerily a good part of the night, didn't help him to feel better.

The following day, around noon, they saw F Station's shape in the distance. Skoll changed clothes and put his uniform, which he had discarded so as not to scare the Iakut, back on. Lien felt even colder just watching him do it without protection from the outside temperature.

As they moved closer, Lien noticed that the tracks were back in place after their long interruption. Skoll told him that there had recently been another huge battle which had been responsible for the damage, the ice had then shifted, erasing all trace of man's activities. Hundreds of bodies had served to feed the marine life that still thrived in the ocean depths beneath the shelf.

Security was in total control of F Station. The Company had installed an autonomous generator to keep the city powered and heated, but it was woefully inadequate. An icy blizzard permanently blew between the railcars, and few people were seen going from one to the other.

The Security guards examined Skoll's papers before allowing them to enter.

"The city's layout has changed," the guard explained. "It used to be a square, about a square mile around, now it's more stretched out over tracks of up to two and a half miles, depending on how many lines it takes up."

They walked until the evening. Periodically, Skoll entered a railcar to ask questions that, more often than not elicited no answers. Little by little, however, they discovered what life was really like in this exiled town. People worked for the army, making uniforms and isothermal suits. In some cars, they cut the patterns; in others they sewed them, before welding the seams to make them totally airtight. The entire town had been turned into a labor camp.

There was a miserable and depressing hotel where they finally ended up at nine o'clock. The atmosphere was dismal, and not lightened by the presence of a few Security Officers drinking beer and vodka. Skoll walked over to greet his colleagues, but was treated coolly with only a few monosyllables in response. In silence, they ate the chewy, tasteless rations which were served to them, not daring to talk so publicly about their preoccupations.

That night, because it was so cold in his room, Lien kept his suit on when he went to bed. He gave a thought to the people in F Station, for whom life was nothing more than this, day after dreary day.

The so-called rebellion that he had heard about in connection with F Station had been nothing more serious than what had occasionally happened in other cities. Yet, F Station had been punished quickly and mercilessly. In addition, the Company had used that opportunity to dump into the mighty canyon of the Bia Sector, its libraries, schools, and anything remotely connected with knowledge, then cover all of it under an immovable mass of ice. There was no doubt in his mind that it had all been part of a plan.

He shared his thoughts with Skoll who slept on the other bunk in their cold, dark room.

"This town was once a thriving intellectual community," the Lieutenant said. "Libzynski was a famous scientist and he'd left his mark here. It attracted others like him, passionate intellectuals always looking to challenge the established dogmas. They'd set up private committees to research the beginning of the ice age, and many more things that we know very little about..."

"But do you know his famous controversial theory, the one about the Ice People's origin?" Lien asked.

"Yes, I do."

Lien waited silently, until Skoll finally added, "If I told it to you now, you wouldn't sleep. So it's better that you don't know, at least not until we get some evidence. It's less dangerous for you, too."

The next day, they followed a tenuous trail that Skoll had uncovered. Libzynski had had some close friends, and Skoll was trying to discover if any of these people, or their families, were still alive. Lien thought they were wasting their time.

"They're probably all dead, or long gone."

Still, since he had nothing better to offer, he followed the Lieutenant in his search. Soon, however, they were rewarded with a modicum of success. One of Libzynski's friends was named Klein, and they found that he had had a son named Len, who had also become a scientist. Unfortunately, further questioning led them to discover that Len Klein was very probably among the dead of the Bia Sector, along with his colleagues and all his pupils. They were back to square one, and feeling very discouraged.

As night fell, they found themselves at the home of an old, deaf woman, whose father had known Libzynski, who had been his neighbor; but she didn't trust them enough to talk freely. To bribe her, they went out and paid a hugely expensive price for a box of sweets which they gave the old woman. That relaxed her, and she began talking more freely.

"Yes, I remember my father talking with him. They often argued about a man called Redd Wolfe."

Lien Rag jumped.

"You mean, the Red Wolf?"

"No, no," she said. "It was a man, named Wolfe, with an 'e'. I saw his name written on a book once; a very old book."

"Yes, it all fits," said Skoll, his eyes shining with excitement, his lips curling up to reveal a set of shiny, white teeth. "What kind of book was it?"

"Some kind of scientific book. I never understood a word of all that stuff, but my father read a lot of scientific books. He loved them."

"Have you kept any of his books? Anything by Redd Wolfe in particular?"

"I don't know. I'll go and look around."

Her suspicions had obviously been rekindled by Skoll's visible excitement. She left her small rail car to go to what she called her "attic", which must have been a storage car nearby.

"Who is this Redd Wolfe? His name doesn't seem to be a mystery to you, Skoll," Lien said.

"We're getting close, Lien, very close!"

They waited, and waited; it felt as if hours were passing by. They were alone in the small, miserable cabin, barely lit by a low watt bulb. In the next cabin, a baby cried, managing to sound like a dying man, almost drowning out the incessant noise of the sewing machines.

Finally, the old woman returned with a big book that she held close to her chest.

"It's one of my father's books. It's worth a lot. Worth a lot."

They understood what she meant, and went out to buy her more food. Eventually, they were able to leave with the book. They took careful precautions to return to the hotel without anyone noticing it. In fact, the saloon room of the hotel was empty when they arrived, but that didn't reassure Skoll.

"Now there's no other alternative for them but to kill us, or make sure we disappear without a trace," he said. "We've got to be very careful. Security must have begun to ask questions about my sudden absence by now. It won't take them long to put it all together. We're in great danger. We'll have dinner and pretend to go to bed, but we'll leave tonight."

"They have our sled."

"It doesn't matter. We'll go north..."

"On foot? That's crazy!"

"Not at all. It's only a day's walk to the Barentz Network. That's the one the Company uses for moving its supplies of fish and they've pretty much managed to keep the Front away from it ever since the war began. But to get there, we'll have to cross a Forbidden Area."

"Forbidden Area? Why? Radioactivity?

"I don't know. I don't have any idea why it's forbidden, or even if it's monitored at all. But if we manage to cross it, we'll get to Norv Station, a small fishing town. We'll smell it from miles around. We'll pose as fish traders..."

"The book, Skoll, can I see the book?"

"Not yet. But you can soon. It's more important than either of our lives, Lien. I'm ready to die for it, but you have to promise me that no matter what happens to me, you'll get it back to civilization and spread its contents."

CHAPTER SEVENTEEN

When dawn rose, they had already traveled a distance that Lien estimated to be twenty to twenty-five miles. They stopped at regular intervals to eat their only food, a kind of very sweet fruit paste that Skoll had purchased.

During their journey, Lien finally learned what Libzynski's controversial theories were. Being a specialist in ancient religions, he had been surprised to find a constant reference to a single deity among all the Ice People, a deity known by diverse variants, depending upon the tribe, but most commonly referred to as the Red Wolf. Somehow, Libzynski had made a connection between that name and that of an obscure geneticist called Redd Wolfe, who had died a hundred years before. Unable to find any information about Wolfe, he had tried to find people who had known him, and from that, to reconstitute the nature of his work. After patient research, he had discovered Wolfe's secret papers, and found that the geneticist's goal was to increase humanity's resistance to cold.

"You mean to tell me that this Redd Wolfe may have created the Redfurs?"

"Exactly. It's all in this book we're carrying. This was what Libzynski found when he arrived at Fiona Station."

"But then the Redfurs are..."

"When they found out about Wolfe, the Companies were very, very worried. They had established their power all over the globe, and that power was based upon man's need to protect himself from the cold. Now, Redd Wolfe appears and shows them that there's another way to achieve the same goal. Needless to say, he was thrown in jail and all traces of his work were destroyed. However, it was too late for the Companies to destroy the Red-furs, who were already living freely upon the ice. The Companies took consolation from the fact that Wolfe's research had not been complete, and that his Ice Men seemed to have only limited intelligence. That had something to do with the lack of some enzyme. The Companies then worked at creating a feeling of racism against the Redfurs, who were shown to be little better than dumb animals. Today, no one could possibly want to live his life the way they do, yet the potential is enormous, beginning with the freedom to roam anywhere on the planet. But, because of the Companies' propaganda, the Redfurs are considered obscene, disgusting, and at best, worthy of pity. Then came Libzynski, who tried to resurrect Redd Wolfe's theories. But they pretended he was crazy, and locked him away..."

They were now climbing down an icy cliff covered with fresh powdered snow. Lien was running out of breath, and was afraid his hood filter had malfunctioned.

"But the Ice People are still here, and they're the living proof that one can survive in the cold. I'm more proof; I can survive outside and my faculties are equal to those of any man. If the Companies knew what I really was, I would be dead."

Later, he told Lien about his plans. He wanted to have Redd Wolfe's book reprinted and circulated to hundreds of biologists and geneticists around the world. This time, no one would be able to suppress the words of the man who had created the Redfurs.

"Wolfe played the sorcerer's apprentice. He took shortcuts. That's why his creations weren't perfect. But by retracing his steps carefully, and improving on his techniques, we can transform man and create a new species able to live freely outside of the domes."

"That would mean the end of the Companies," Lien said. "They'll never stand for it."

"If thousands of people in thousands of different places know, how could they stop it? We'll also expose the Trans-European's role in the massacre of F Station. I have evidence. We'll make it, you'll see."

Lien had reached the top of another ice cliff and stopped in surprise. In front of him lay a vast plain surrounded by more cliffs; but instead of being covered in ice and snow, it was verdant, dotted with darker, almost black, spots, here and there.

"What is it?" he asked in amazement.

"Vegetation. Natural vegetation," Skoll replied, moved by the sight of such an unusual spectacle. "And the air is warm. I feel it on my face. Take off your hood."

Lien waited carefully for a few minutes, but suddenly understood that it was the warm outside air that had created in his mind the idea that his filter might be malfunctioning.

"The temperature is above forty here, the ice cliffs have begun to melt. This plain probably grows a few feet larger every year."

From the blackened spots, he noticed wisps of smoke which provided the explanation for the strange phenomenon.

"It's because of volcanic activity. That's why it's listed as a Forbidden Area. The Company is afraid that outsiders will come to live here."

Descent onto the plain was not easy, because of the cliffs' steepness. They walked for hours seeking a passageway leading down. Finally, they found a narrow one, but it smelled horribly, and Lien was forced to put his hood back on. Soon after, they discovered rotting carcasses of dead animals at the bottom.

"Carbon monoxide," Lien said. "It's frequent in volcanic areas. They were all asphyxiated."

Skoll himself was beginning to pass out, but was saved by Lien vigorously pulling him out of the crevice, and placing the hood of the other suit over his face. The hood's filters appeared to stop the gas.

"Thank you," the Lieutenant whispered. "Now I understand why the Company doesn't bother keeping a watch on this place. The only access is naturally pro- tected."

"It's going to be hard to make it with all these putrefying bodies."

"We have to. We'll find some hot water on the oth- er side, I'm sure, and we'll wash up carefully then. Let's try it."

They had to move several rotting wolf carcasses out of the way. The wolves must have been chasing a herd of reindeer when they all fell into the passage. Their bo- dies were now almost welded together by putrefaction. The more the men pulled, the more the bodies disinte- grated. One of the reindeer, bloated by gasses, exploded, showering them with a foul rain of rotten flesh and ex- crement. They became frenzied in their desire to reach the other side of the charnel pit and worked even harder.

They almost fell prey to discouragement, thinking they would be stuck forever and die there, when they came across a layer of Redfur bodies, all members of a tribe which must have been drawn to the valley and then died here. There were about twenty of them, men, wom- en and children, all lying amalgamated together in a hor- rible mass. But these were the last.

When they reached the other side, they felt as if they had been vomited up by some giant organism. They ran towards a pool of water and began washing themselves, panting and almost hysterical.

Later, they started across the volcanic plain, carefully avoiding the craters and geysers which littered the place.

"With the proper equipment, a hundred thousand people could live here happily," Skoll said.

Lien was deep in thought as to how they were going to cross on the other side. Were they going to have to repeat the same experience in another passage? And would they even be able to find one?

Suddenly, they noticed a small animal, which looked a little like a miniature reindeer.

"Either there's another passage, or else some animals were able to make it before the one we took got blocked."

"Could any men have made it too?"

"I don't know. I guess anything's possible."

Night was falling and they had found no other passage, only tracks left by some animals which they guessed to be descendents of horses.

"I think we should spend the night here," Skoll said, sitting on a lichen-covered rock.

Lichen made up most of the valley's vegetation, along with a few dwarf trees and some grass. In spots, they had noticed plants that looked something like wheat. Maybe some seeds had been carried to this forsaken place by the wind, and had miraculously taken root.

They slept next to a warm spring. In the middle of the night, Lien got up to urinate, and suddenly noticed a light in the far distance. He ran to wake up Skoll.

They decided to investigate immediately. As they got nearer, they heard shouting and dogs barking. Skoll smiled.

"They're Iakut! We're saved!"

It was a family that had fled here following a fight with the Company's local representatives. They planned to raise reindeer here, and live happily ever after. They told Skoll that they had arrived there by crossing what they called the "fire lake." As far as they knew, it was the only way in.

At dawn, two of the men took them there. It was a lake of boiling water and sulfuric emanations; according to the Iakut, it was a mile long, surrounded by two steep ice cliffs, which it was eroding, inch by inch. Sometimes, a chunk of ice fell into the water, causing huge waves capable of capsizing their small boats.

There were three reindeer skin canoes on the beach, and the perspective of crossing the lake in one of them didn't thrill Lien; neither he nor Skoll had any boating experience. Only very rich people like Floa could afford to learn this useless skill, in places like the club.

Getting the Iakut to sell them a boat wasn't easy. Money was useless here and, at first, they refused. It was only when Lien pulled huge wads of bank notes from his pockets that they began to change their minds. After all, a day might arrive when they would need some cash to trade with the outside world.

Lien began to panic when they reached the middle of the lake; the water was bubbling furiously and, without the protection of their hoods, they would have already been suffocated. It was a wonder that the Iakut had made it at all. He couldn't believe that the frail canoe would make it for the rest of the journey and truly felt that they were going to die there, in the hellish cauldron.

But Skoll kept the skiff on a steady course, and an hour later they reached an ice shelf that was being gradually eaten away by the water. They jumped ashore, and Lien noticed that they could never have gone back, because the bottom of the canoe had been more than half dissolved by the acidic water.

In the afternoon, they saw Norv Station ahead of them and, as Skoll had promised, they began to smell the rancid odor of fish. Their journey was over.

Three days later, in River Station, the dwarf who was Cabaret Mikki's stage manager couldn't believe his nose. He was standing in front of the Cabaret, dressed in a joker's costume, barking the numerous attractions of the place to tempt passers-by to enter, when he smelled a strong odor of fish.

He looked at a man who stood not more than two feet away.

"Say, sailor, it's not an aquarium here. You... Wait a minute, I recognize you. You're Yeuse's friend, aren't you?"

"Yes," Lien said. "Is she here? I need to see her. It's an emergency."

The dwarf looked around suspiciously.

"She's being watched by Security, but I'll see what I can do."

Following his advice, Lien had to crawl under the car and use a secret trapdoor to gain access to the Cabaret's backstage. From there, it was easy to find Yeuse's dressing room; in spite of his pungent smell, nobody questioned him.

"My god, it's you!" she said.

She hugged him, and almost immediately shrank back because of the smell.

"I had to travel in a freight car full of fish," Lien apologized.

"You shouldn't have come back here," Yeuse said. "Floa reached an agreement with Security. Now, she's a little bit richer; ten percent more stock, at no cost."

"You mean; she sold me out?"

Yeuse closed her eyes.

"I hate to say this, but I don't think she had any choice. She may even have calculated that you would become a valuable commodity, and she could use you to strike a deal with Security. Who knows? But you can't stay here. She comes over almost every night, and I know the Cabaret's under surveillance. Did you find F Station?"

He nodded.

"What are you going to do?"

"I'm leaving for Grand Star Station. I'm not alone anymore. There are others who are fighting for freedom against the Company. When I can, I'll join you, wherever you are."

Yeuse smiled weakly, fighting back tears.

"Soon, you'll get a book in the mail," he told her. "An amazing book. We're going to have it printed and circulated to as many people as we can. Its author was a man named Redd Wolfe..."

"If it comes from you, I'll read it of course. What's it called?"

"*The Oblique Road.*"

THE END

PUBLISHING HISTORY

Volumes 1 to 36 of *The Ice Company* were published in the regular *Anticipation* imprint of Editions Fleuve Noir. As was the practice at the time, the cover art was randomly purchased from a number of British studios (mostly VLOO - Young Artists), and did not particularly reflect the contents of the books.

1. La Compagnie des Glaces [*The Ice Company*] (*Anticip.* No. 997, 1980 / reprinted in Omnibus No. 1)
2. Le Sanctuaire des Glaces [*The Ice Sanctuary*] (*Anticip.* No. 1038, 1981 / Omnibus 1)
3. Le Peuple des Glaces [*The Ice People*] (*Anticip.* No. 1056, 1981 / Omnibus 1)
4. Les Chasseurs des Glaces [*The Ice Hunters*] (*Anticip.* No. 1077, 1981 / Omnibus 1)
5. L'Enfant des Glaces [*The Ice Child*] (*Anticip.* No. 1104, 1981 / reprinted in Omnibus No. 2)
6. Les Otages des Glaces [*The Ice Hostages*] (*Anticip.* No. 1116, 1982 / Omnibus 2)
7. Le Gnome Halluciné [*The Visionary Dwarf*] (*Anticip.* No. 1122, 1982 / Omnibus 2)
8. La Compagnie de la Banquise [*The Pacific Shelf Company*] (*Anticip.* No. 1139, 1982 / Omnibus 2)
9. Le Réseau de Patagonie [*The Patagonia Network*] (*Anticip.* No. 1157, 1982 / reprinted in Omnibus No. 3)
10. Les Voiliers du Rail [*The Rail Sailboats*] (*Anticip.* No. 1180, 1982 / Omnibus 3)
11. Les Fous du Soleil [*The Sun Fanatics*] (*Anticip.* No. 1198, 1983 / Omnibus 3)

ANTICIPATION

G.-J. ARNAUD

LES ÉBOUEURS
DE LA VIE ÉTERNELLE

La Compagnie des Glaces

fleuve noir

12. Network-Cancer [*Cancer Network*] (*Anticip.* No. 1207, 1983 / Omnibus 3)

13. Station-Fantôme [*Ghost Station*] (*Anticip.* No. 1224, 1983 / reprinted in Omnibus No. 4)

14. Les Hommes-Jonas [*The Jonah Men*] (*Anticip.* No. 1249, 1983 / Omnibus 4)

15. Terminus Amertume [*Terminus Despair*] (*Anticip.* No. 1267, 1983 / Omnibus 4)

16. Les Brûleurs de Banquise [*The Ice Melters*] (*Anticip.* No. 1271, 1984 / Omnibus 4)

17. Le Gouffre aux Garous [*The Were-Pit*] (*Anticip.* No. 1286, 1984 / reprinted in Omnibus No. 5)

18. Le Dirigeable Sacrilège [*The Sacrilegious Airship*] (*Anticip.* No. 1303, 1984 / Omnibus 5)

19. Liensun (*Anticip.* No. 1321, 1984 / Omnibus 5)

20. Les Éboueurs de la Vie Éternelle [*The Dumpsters Of Eternity*] (*Anticip.* No. 1333, 1984 / Omnibus 5)

21. Les Trains Cimetières [*The Graveyard Trains*] (*Anticip.* No. 1351, 1985 / reprinted in Omnibus No. 6)

22. Les Fils de Lien Rag [*The Sons of Lien Rag*] (*Anticip.* No. 1364, 1985 / Omnibus 6)

23. Voyageuse Yeuse [*Voyager Yeuse*] (Anticip. No. 1388, 1985 / Omnibus 6)

24. L'Ampoule de Cendres [*The Glass Urn*] (Anticip. No. 1405, 1985 / Omnibus 6)

25. Sun Company (*Anticip.* No. 1431, 1986 / Omnibus 7)

26. Les Sibériens [*The Siberians*] (*Anticip.* No. 1449, 1986 / reprinted in Omnibus No. 7)

27. Le Clochard Ferroviaire [*The Mysterious Hobo*] (*Anticip.* No. 1460, 1986 / Omnibus 7)

28. Les Wagons Mémoires [*The Memory Trains*] (*Anticip.* No. 1477, 1986 / Omnibus 7)

29. Mausolée pour une Locomotive [*The Fabulous Locomotive*] (*Anticip.* No. 1490, 1986 / reprinted in Omnibus No. 8)

30. Dans le Ventre d'une Légende [*In The Belly Of A Legend*] (*Anticip.* No. 1503, 1986 / Omnibus 8)

31. Les Échafaudages d'Épouvante [*The Scaffolds Of Fear*] (Anticip. No. 1516, 1987 / Omnibus 8)

32. Les Montagnes Affamées [*The Hungry Mountains*] (*Anticip.* No. 1541, 1987 / Omnibus 8)

33. La Prodigieuse Agonie [*The Prodigious Agony*] (Anticip. No. 1552, 1987 / reprinted in Omnibus No. 9)

34. On m'appelait Lien Rag [*They Called Me Lien Rag*] (*Anticip.* No. 1571, 1987 / Omnibus 9)

35. Train Spécial Pénitentiaire 34 [*Special Penitentiary Train 34*] (*Anticip.* No. 1581, 1987 / Omnibus 9)

36. Les Hallucinés de la Voie Oblique [*The Madmen Of The Oblique Road*] (*Anticip.* No. 1596, 1987 / Omnibus 9)

In 1988, *The Ice Company* was awarded its own dedicated imprint, with blue covers sporting illustrations by Patrick Demuth.

Volumes 37 to 62 were originally published in that imprint, which also simultaneously reprinted Volumes 1 to 36, bringing the series to a temporary conclusion with Volume 62 in 1992.

37. L'Abominable Postulat [*The Abominable Verdict*] (*CDG* No. 37, 1988 / reprinted Omnibus No. 10)

38. Le Sang des Ragus [*The Blood of the Ragus*] (CDG No. 38, 1988 / Omnibus 10)

39. La Caste des Aiguilleurs [*The Dispatchers Guild*] (*CDG* No. 39, 1988 / Omnibus 10)

G.-J. ARNAUD

LA COMPAGNIE DES GLACES

38

Le sang des Ragus

ANTICIPATION
FLEUVE NOIR

40. Les Exilés du Ciel Croûteux [*The Castaways of a Crusty Sky*] (*CDG* No. 40, 1988 / Omnibus 10)

41. Exode Barbare [*Savage Exodus*] (*CDG* No. 41, 1988 / Omnibus 11)

42. La Chair des Étoiles [*The Flesh of the Stars*] (*CDG* No. 42, 1988 / reprinted in Omnibus No. 11)

43. L'Aube Cruelle d'un Temps Nouveau [*The Bloody Dawn of the New Times*] (*CDG* No. 43, 1988 / Omnibus 11)

44. Les Canyons du Pacifique [*The Canyons of the Pacific*] (*CDG* No. 44, 1989 / Omnibus 11)

45. Les Vagabonds des Brumes [*The Wanderers In The Mist*] (*CDG* No. 45, 1989 / reprinted in Omnibus No. 12)

46. La Banquise Déchiquetée [*The Wrecked Ice Shelf*] (*CDG* No. 46, 1989 / Omnibus 12)

47. Soleil Blême [*Wan Sun*] (*CDG* No. 47, 1989 / Omnibus 12)

48. L'Huile des Morts [*The Oil of the Dead*] (*CDG* No. 48, 1989 / Omnibus 12)

49. Les Oubliés de Chimère [*The Forsakens of Chimera*] (*CDG* No. 49, 1989 / reprinted Omnibus No. 13)

50. Les Cargos-Dirigeables du Soleil [*The Airships of the Sun*] (*CDG* No. 50, 1990 / Omnibus 13)

51. La Guilde des Sanguinaires [*The Bloody Guild*] (*CDG* No. 51, 1990 / Omnibus 13)

52. La Croix Pirate [*The Pirate Cross*] (*CDG* No. 52, 1990 / Omnibus 13)

53. Le Pays de Djoug [*The Land of Djoug*] (*CDG* No. 53, 1990 / reprinted in Omnibus No. 14)

54. La Banquise de Bois [*The Pontoons of Lacustra*] (*CDG* No. 54, 1990 / Omnibus 14)

55. Iceberg-Ship (*CDG* No. 55, 1991 / Omnibus 14)

56. Lacustra City (CDG No. 56, 1991 / Omnibus 14)

57. L'Héritage du Bulb [*The Bulb's Inheritance*] (*CDG* No. 57, 1991 / reprinted in Omnibus No. 15)

58. Les Millénaires Perdus [*The Lost Millenia*] (*CDG* No. 58, 1991 / Omnibus 15)

59. La Guerre du Peuple du Froid [*The War of the Ice People*] (*CDG* No. 59, 1991 / Omnibus 15)

60. Les Tombeaux de l'Antarctique [*The Tombs of Antarctica*] (*CDG* No. 60, 1992 / Omnibus 15)

61. La Charogne Céleste [*The Cosmic Remains*] (*CDG* No. 61, 1992 / reprinted in Omnibus No. 16)

62. Il Était Une Fois La Compagnie Des Glaces [*Once Upon A Time, The Ice Company*] (*CDG* No. 62, 1992 / Omnibus 16)

The entire series was reprinted again in a 16-volume omnibus series, each collecting four of the original novels, sporting covers by Philippe Jozelon.

The last omnibus volume (Volume 16) contained a new novel, written especially for that book, and an Encyclopedia of the Ice Company Universe, compiled by Noé Gaillard.

61b. L'Avenir des Dupes [*The Dupes' Future*] (Omnibus 16, 2000)

In 1996, Arnaud began the *Chroniques Glaciaires* series *(The Ice Chronicles)*, which recounted untold tales of the past history of the universe of the Ice Company. The first volume was again published by Fleuve Noir in their *Anticipation* imprint.

1. Les Rails d'Incertitude [*The Rails of Uncertainty*] (*Anticip.* No. 1995, 1996)

G.-J. Arnaud

LA COMPAGNIE DES GLACES

XVI

UN ÉPISODE INÉDIT

FLEUVE NOIR

SF METAL

G.-J. ARNAUD

Les Illuminés

FLEUVE NOIR

The second and third volumes of The Ice Chronicles were published in Fleuve Noir's new *SF Métal* imprint, launched after the cancellation of Anticipation, featuring cover art by Jean-Yves Kervévan).

Finally, *The Ice Chronicles* were granted their own dedicated imprint, with covers by Philippe Jozelon, with Volume 4 in 1999.

2. Les Illuminés [*The Illuminated*] (*Métal* No. 26, 1997)
3. Le Sang du Monde [*The Blood of the World*] (*Métal* No. 36, 1998)

4. Les Prédestinés [*The Predestined*] (FNCHR 4, 1999)
5. Les Survivants Crépusculaires [*The Twilight Survivors*] (FNCHR 5, 1999)
6. Sidéral Léviathan (FNCHR 6, 1999)
7. L'Oeil Parasite [*The Parasitic Eye*] (FNCHR 7, 1999)
8. Planète Nomade [*Nomadic Planet*] (FNCHR 8, 2000)
9. Roark (FNCHR 9, 2000)
10. Les Baleines Solinas [*The Solinas Whales*] (FNCHR 10, 2000)
11. La Légende des Hommes-Jonas [*The Legend Of The Jonah Men*] (FNCHR 11, 2001)

G.-J. Arnaud

LA LÉGENDE
DES HOMMES-JONAS

CHRONIQUES **XI** GLACIAIRES

FLEU
VE
NOIR

L'UNIVERS DE
LA COMPAGNIE
DES GLACES

Finally, in 2001, Fleuve Noir launched a second series of *Ice Company* novels in its own dedicated imprint, entitled *Nouvelle Epoque* (*New Era*), taking place 15 years after the end of the first series. The covers were, again, the work of Philippe Jozelon..

1. La Ceinture de Feu [*The Fire Belt*] (*NE* No. 1, 2001)
2. Le Chenal Noir [*The Dark Channel*] (*NE* No. 2 2, 2001)
3. Le Réseau de l'Éternelle Nuit [*The Network of Eternal Night*] (*NE* No. 3, 2001)
4. Les Hommes du Cauchemar [*The Nightmare Men*] (CDG No.2 4, 2001)
5. Les Spectres de l'Altiplano [*The Ghosts of the Altiplano*] (*NE* No. 5, 2001)
6. Les Momies du Massacre [*The Mummies from the Massacre*] (*NE* No. 6, 2002)
7. L'Ombre du Serpent Gris [*The Shadow of the Grey Snake*] (*NE* No. 7, 2002)
8. Les Griffes de la Banquise [*The Claws of the Ice Shelf*] (*NE* No. 8, 2002)
9. Les Forbans du Nord [*The Northern Pirates*] (*NE* No. 9, 2002)
10. Les Icebergs Lunaires [*Icebergs from the Moon*] (*NE* No. 10, 2002)
11. Le Sanctuaire de Légende [*The Legendary Sanctuary*] (*NE* No. 11, 2002)
12. Les Mystères d'Altaï [*The Mysteries of Altai*] (*NE* No. 12, 2003)
13. La Locomotive-Dieu [*The God-Locomotive*] (*NE* No. 13, 2003)
14. Pari Cataclysme [*Cataclysm Bet*] (*NE* No. 14, 2003)
15. Movane la Chamane [*Movane the Shaman*] (CDG No.2 15, 2003)

16. Channel Drake [*Drake Channel*] (*NE* No. 16, 2003)
17. Le Sang des Aliens [*The Blood of Aliens*] (*NE* No. 17, 2004)
18. Caste Barbare [*Barbarian Caste*] (*NE* No. 18, 2004)
19. Parano River (*NE* No. 19, 2004)
20. Indomptable Fleur [*Indomitable Flower*] (*NE* No. 20, 2004)
21. Le Masque de l'autre [*The Other's Mask*] (*NE* No. 21, 2005)
22. Passions rapaces [*Ravening Passions*] (*NE* No. 22, 2005)
23. L'Irrévocable testament [*The Irrevocable Testament*] (*NE* No. 23, 2006)
24. Ultime Mirage [*Last Mirage*] (*NE* No. 24, 2006)

G.-J. ARNAUD
LA COMPAGNIE DES GLACES
1
Nouvelle
époque
La Ceinture de Feu
FLEU
VE
NOIR

OVERVIEW OF THE SERIES [1]

The Ice Company series is the sprawling saga of a future Earth that lives in a new Ice Age.

When the series begins, Earth's population is living in domed cities, connected by extended rail networks, which carry power as well as food, trains, etc. These networks are controlled by powerful, oligarchic rail companies which, effectively, rule the world.

As we later learn, the new Ice Age came about when the Moon exploded, and the resulting cosmic debris surrounded the Earth and blocked all of the Sun's light. Civilization collapsed, and after several centuries of barbarism, the age of the Ice Companies eventually arose.

The Earth of *The Ice Company* is ruled by a variety of powerful, often secret, organizations, such as:

* the autocratic Dispatchers Guild, who holds the keys to the origins of the Ice Companies;

* the manipulative Church the Neo-Catholics, who also control pre-Ice Age secrets which might disturb the new society;

* the Sun Reclaimers, a fanatical sect of mystics and scientists trying to scatter the Moondust and bring about the return of the Sun, no matter what havoc it may cause;

---

[1] The following presentation was initially written in 1987 to accompany the translation of Volume 1, and included summaries of Volumes 1 to 34 only. The introduction, however, was updated to the start of the *New Era* in 2000.

* the Jonah Men, a secretive new race of men who have evolved to live inside giant sperm whales;

* the Simone, a small band of dwarfish humanoids whose ghost-like, nuclear-powered ship roams the Pacific Sea; and many more.

The most tantalizing mystery of all is the existence, on the ice shelf, of tribes of red-furred humanoids, who can stand the freezing cold, and whose origins are, at first, a baffling enigma.

A scientist, Lien Rag, embarks on an odyssey to discover the secret origins of his world. As the series progresses, other major characters are established:

* the Kid, or the Gnome, a resourceful dwarf who later founds the powerful Ice Shelf Company on top of the frozen Pacific;

* Yeuse, the beautiful, former cabaret singer who eventually climbs to a position of power as Lady Diana's heir;

* Kurts the pirate, a mutant with a powerful computerized rogue locomotive;

* Lady Diana, the head of the Transamerican Company and one of the few persons to know the secrets origins of the companies;

* Lienty Ragus, or Gus, Lien Rag's adventurous but legless cousin.

Lien Rag eventually fathers two sons: Jdrien, a half-human, half redfur, and the enterprising Liensun.

Lien's quest eventually takes him through the so-called *Oblique Road* into space, where all the secrets of his world are at last revealed on a giant, space-faring sentient ship orbiting the Earth, the Bulb.

Lien discovers that, prior to the destruction of the Moon, Earth colonists migrated to the planet Ophiuchus IV. The colony failed, and some of the colonists eventually returned to Earth in the Bulb. They split into two sections: One, the Ragus—Lien's ancestors—who tried to help Earth. The other, the Dispatchers' ancestors, who decided to preserve the Ice Age and were responsible for the genetic creation of the Redfurs.

Reclaiming Earth from its frozen state then becomes the focus of Lien Rag's adventures, after his return to Earth, ten years after he left it. (There is a ten-year gap between Volumes 20 and 21 of the series.)

This is ultimately achieved when a band of Sun Reclaimers manage to break up the Moondust.

The world suffers through a new economic collapse, as the ice companies are forced to evolve or disappear. Old powers crumble, new alliances form, and various wars erupt around the globe. The Bulb eventually crashes down to Earth, triggering new cataclysmic changes. Some old characters die, while new ones are introduced.

Finally, a temporary peace of sorts is reached in Volume 62, when the Northern and Southern hemispheres are cut off from each other by a fiery belt of unfiltered sunlight at the Equator.

But, 15 years later, when the *New Era* begins, a new alliance composed of the Dispatchers and the Neo-Catholics plots to recreate the Ice World. Lien, Yeuse, and Lien's grandson (descended from Jdrien), the half-breed Jdriege, face new challenges...

The Books

1: The Ice Company:

In the TRANS-EUROPEAN COMPANY, glaciologist LIEN RAG and his crew are sent to an isolated site where they witness the massacre of thousands of people who had rebelled against the Company. When Lien tries to tell what he's seen, he is arrested by MAJOR VICRA of Military Security, and thrown into jail.

But Lien is rescued by FLOA, the beautiful daughter of GOVERNOR SADON, and a powerful Company shareholder. Floa uses Lien in her own political war against Security, which acts as a front for the NEO-CATHOLIC CHURCH which is trying to gain control of the Company. But after being frightened by the Church's BROTHER PETER, she abandons Lien.

Lien then begins his investigation of the origins of the mysterious Ice People known as "REDFURS." His research pits him against Security Lieutenant SKOLL but, undaunted, Lien meets with scientist HAL MERN, who gives him precious clues. These lead him to discover the existence of a mythical geneticist named REDD WOLFE, who may have created the Redfurs in an experiment to help Mankind adapt to the cold. With the help of YEUSE, a dancer at the CABARET MIKKI, Lien finds his way to the Front, where a fierce war is being waged between the Trans-European and the SIBERIAN, to find new evidence. There, again he meets SKOLL, who turns out to be a Human/Redfur halfbreed. Together, they locate a book written by Wolfe called "The Oblique Road," which they plan to reprint and circulate.

2: The Ice Sanctuary:

KURTS, a pirate who commands a gigantic loco-motive able to travel anywhere freely, kidnaps Floa for ransom. Floa's father contacts Lien, who is now hiding with Skoll at the zoo managed by Mern, and tells him that he doesn't trust the Company to pay her ransom. Instead, he wants Lien to handle it and, in exchange, of-fers to give him a map pinpointing the location of Redd Wolfe's secret laboratory.

Later, Lien once again meets Yeuse, then Brother Peter, with whom he has more conversations about the Redfurs' secret origin. Meanwhile, Security arrests Skoll. Thanks to the Governor's help, Lien, Mern and Yeuse manage to escape and set off to deliver the ran-som to a far western location designated by Kurts.

There, they meet a tribe of intelligent, armed Ice People whose CHIEF is Kurts' blood brother. Finally, they meet Kurts himself, who also turns out to be a halfbreed. Floa, who has become Kurts' lover, refuses to leave but he sends her away. Lien is given the promised map and, leaving Mern behind, embarks on a grueling polar trip during which he encounters WERE-BEASTS: wolves with human faces -- possibly the results of Wolfe's earlier experiments.

Eventually, he arrives at an isolated Neo-Catholic monastery where he again meets Brother Peter. The mis-sionary wants Lien, who refuses, to lead him to Wolfe's lab. However, when he arrives at the site, he finds it de-stroyed. Brother Peter has preceded him on a fuel-powered sled. Later, Peter tells Lien he considers he did the Neo-Catholics a favor by helping them locate and destroy the lab, so that when Lien returns to the Compa-ny, he receives both a pardon and a promotion.

3: The Ice People:

A Trans-European commando is attacked by a tribe of armed Redfurs near the PAN-AMERICAN frontier, which the Company then declares forbidden area. But Lien Rag, who has been sent to study the Northern Atlantic ice shelf in preparation for a war between the Trans-European and the Pan-American, discovers its secret.

Security Major LONDAL frees Skoll, and asks him, along with Lien and Mern, to investigate the Redfurs situation. At first, they go to live among a peaceful, primitive tribe, where Lien falls in love with JDROU, a beautiful female. Later, they meet the "civilized" Redfurs, who have been armed by Kurts. Their hope is to create a free WESTERN ZONE for their brethren. Lien and Mern discover that the Neo-Catholic Church has secretly been educating the Redfurs, even as they hate-monger against them in the Cities. In this way, they plan to regain the momentum they lost after Floa defeated their attempt to take-over the Company.

Skoll decides to remain with his people, while Lien and Mern return to Londal, who is unable to counterattack because the ice shelf has been cleverly booby-trapped by the Pan-Americans. If Lien will help solve the problem, the Major will let him look for Jdrou. Interracial violence reaches its peak, and the Redfurs leave the Cities en masse; man begins hunting them like animals.

In the midst of this chaos, Lien finds Jdrou and they make love. He decides to desert, and takes her, and her tribe, to a lonely timber farm managed by a man named HANSEN.

4: The Ice Hunters:

Life at the timber farm is peaceful. One day, Lien learns that the Cabaret Mikki has stopped in a nearby Station. He meets with Yeuse, who warns him against wild packs of ICE HUNTERS. When Lien returns to the farm, he finds that Hansen's WIFE has been raped and Jdrou's tribe captured; he sets out to find her.

The Redfur slaving program is in full force in the Trans-European Company. Thousands of captured Redfurs are branded, treated like animals and forced to work for the Company; Mern has been drafted because of his knowledge of Redfurs. Meanwhile, Lien has managed to find the hunters who kidnapped Jdrou, but Hansen has caught up with them too and murders several of them. Although the woodsman escapes, Lien is arrested; he is thrown in jail and condemned to six years hard labor.

Meanwhile, Jdrou has been sent to Mern's camp, where he recognizes her, and discovers she is pregnant. His research leads him to the conclusion that Redfurs may be artificial creations, but cannot be Redd Wolfe's, because his work was too recent and there are too many of them. Some colleagues advance the theory that the Redfurs possibly came from Outer Space. Later, Mern is unable to intervene when Jdrou is sent east to a station called PURPLE STATION.

Three months later, Floa visits Lien and tells him that she is powerless to have him freed, but Kurts is on the warpath against the Hunters. Yeuse, however, manages to arrange Lien's escape with the help of Hansen and the DWARF from Cabaret Mikki. Lien then joins the troupe and poses as a Redfur. When he arrives in Purple Station, he finds Jdrou, who has just given birth to his son: JDRIEN.

5: The Ice Child:

Lien now leads a difficult life with Jdrou and Jdrien, among the Redfurs, in Purple Station. Meanwhile, the Station where Yeuse has been performing is attacked by Western Zone Redfurs and Were-beasts. To hush it up, Security deports the Cabaret Mikki to the Front. Meanwhile, Jdrou's tribe leaves, abandoning Lien and Jdrien.

Lien tries to locate Yeuse, but fails. He ends up in SALT STATION where he becomes a miner. There, he befriends VAK, a member of the secret sect of the SUN RECLAIMERS, who look for ways to bring about the return of the sun. Vak is at work on an ultra-sound device which could blast a hole in the lunar dust cloud that surrounds the Earth; but the consequences would be terrifying: melted ice would cover the globe in water.

Eventually, Lien finds a member of Jdrou's tribe and learns she was killed by a Hunter; he kills her murderer, but must flee to NORV STATION, where he becomes a fisherman. There, Jdrien begins to display strange mental powers. Meanwhile, after a gruesome life at the Front, Yeuse is given a leave and succeeds in tracking down Lien.

She arrives just as all Redfurs mysteriously leave Norv Station, thus endangering the fishermen's livelihood; a mob threatens to lynch Lien. Yeuse takes Jdrien with her to save his life, and returns to the Front just as the Siberians attack and capture the Cabaret. Meanwhile, Security offers to save Lien if he will betray Vak. Brother Peter later offers him the same deal, which he refuses. As all seems lost, he is rescued by Kurts.

6: The Ice Hostages:

Skoll has sent Kurts to save Lien's life. Now, they must return to the Western Zone. The fabulous locomotive travels south to the Mediterranean ice shelf, battling the Trans-European's forces, then heads north into Pan-American territory on the Atlantic Ice Shelf. Meanwhile, Cabaret Mikki performs for the Siberian military an Yeuse becomes the mistress of COLONEL SOFI, a fierce, powerful Cossack warrior.

Once in the Western Zone, Lien learns that Skoll wants him to go to the Pan-Americans to be a spy. Once there, he is interrogated by FUERZA, a member of the Pan-American Security, who knows all about his past, and is concerned by his connections with the Sun Reclaimers. However, his experience as a glaciologist enables him to be freed to start working on an ambitious East-West ice tunnel.

Lien meets LADY DIANA, a fat, powerful Pan-American Board member. Later, he performs an engineering feat to free an old tanker caught under the ice, which makes him a hero. He is then able to convince Lady Diana to support the Western Zone, since it would be to the detriment of Trans-European. In exchange, she will gain their support against her enemies: the Sun Reclaimers.

Meanwhile, Cabaret Mikki is forced to flee a Trans-European counter-attack by taking a hellish ride deep into Siberian territory. Yeuse kills an officer who tries to rape her, is arrested and condemned to twenty years in a penitentiary train. She entrusts Jdrien to the Dwarf and another dancer, MIELE, who set out on a course through South East Asia. Lien, who has used his new status to get information about them, makes a deal with Lady Diana: he will work on her newest project, a North Pole-South Pole tunnel, if she rescues Yeuse and Jdrien.

7: *The Visionary Dwarf:*

The Dwarf, Jdrien (whom he now treats as a son) and Miele and Jdrien find refuge in a Station ruled by GENERAL CHERAKINE, an old Siberian dying from gangrene. Jdrien's mental powers help relieve the General, who no longer wants to let them leave. So the Dwarf must travel south into the AUSTRALASIAN COMPANIES to bring back medication.

Meanwhile, Lien has become a powerful figure in the Pan-American, and is preparing to begin work on the North-South Tunnel. This makes the Dwarf, who has heard about his success, even more determined to keep Jdrien with him. Fuerza eventually locates Yeuse's penitentiary train, and Lien literally buys her back from the Siberians. But she finds she no longer loves him and returns to the Trans-European to continue her dancing career. While Lady Diana pursues her war against the Sun Reclaimers, Lien desperately tries to discover Jdrien's whereabouts.

Eventually, General Cherakine dies, leaving his fortune to Jdrien. The Dwarf flees with the child and Miele, who has become his mistress, to the Australasian, where he uses the money to buy a small, bankrupt rail company, the S.N.O.W., which he rechristens the KID, which also becomes his new nickname. Eventually, he forges a business alliance with the MIKADO, a repulsively fat sybarite tycoon, who is also a secret half-breed.

The Dwarf then travels alone far out onto the vast and terrifying Pacific Ice Shelf where almost no man has gone before, and finds a huge volcano which could provide limitless energy. He decides to create a new Com-

pany that will one day rival the others: the PACIFIC
SHELF COMPANY.

8: The Pacific Shelf Company:
    In KAMENEPOLIS, the capital of the new Pacific
Shelf Company, the Kid is facing economic difficulties
and the opposition of the WHALERS. Against his better
judgment, he is forced to create a police force, headed by
WALKER; new immigrants and political troublemakers
are to be sent to a new Station on the outskirts of the
Company, nicknamed DESPAIR STATION.
    Later, the Kid meets with Yeuse, who has been
drawn to the new Company by rumors. The Kid, who
loves Jdrien, does not want to let him go; he wants to
build an empire to show the child he is better than Lien.
But civil strife erupts, and WALKER stages a coup. He
is secretly financed by Lady Diana, who has sent an
agent, LEWIS, to kidnap Jdrien.
    Lien is now working in Patagonia on the new
North-South Tunnel. Lady Diana's decision to draw on
all the area's available power by pretending there is a
malfunction, causes over one million deaths. Disgusted,
Lien stops working and is sent to the Western Zone to
negotiate a trade agreement. There, he acquires a new
lover, the beautiful half-breed LOUAN.
    Meanwhile, the Kid uses superior strategic skills
and Jdrien's influence over the Redfurs to unseat Walker
an Yeuse shoots Lewis as he tries to kidnap Jdrien. The
Kid now knows Lady Diana is his enemy. Meanwhile,
further north, a secret group of Sun Reclaimers, led by
JULIUS and MA KERR, by using a laser, finally succeed in blasting a small hole in the dust cloud that surrounds the Earth. For the first time in centuries, a brief,
but frightening burst of sun is seen all across the Pacific.

9: The Patagonia Network:

Skoll tells Lien about the horrible things he has heard are happening in Patagonia. Lien and Louan decide to travel there to find out the truth. Petitions have reached the CANYST (The Commission for the Application of the New York Station Treaty), the 8-member "United Nations" of the world. They decide to send a Commission and give Lady Diana eight days to have the Patagonia Network re-electrified.

Meanwhile, the Kid decides to apply for membership in the CANYST, and sends Yeuse as his ambassador. He also learns about a Redfur prophecy proclaiming Jdrien as the future leader of the Ice People. The mystery of the Redfurs' origin deepens as the Kid discovers that the story of Redd Wolfe's story was mostly fabricated by the Neo-Catholic Church, which holds secret documents about the Redfurs, possibly pre-dating the Ice Age.

In Patagonia, Lien betrays Lady Diana and, instead of covering up for her, reveals to the CANYST Commission that there was no accident. The power has been diverted for the North-South tunnel. Then, they find that all the Stations are empty of bodies, alive or dead. Eventually, Lien discovers the horrible truth: Lady Diana has had the Patagonian population poisoned to use the corpses as fuel in her power stations. Before the Commission has the chance to take action, they are murdered by Diana's agents. Only Lien, Louan and KAPOUL, the Africanian commissioner, manage to escape.

In the Pacific Shelf Company, the Kid decides to create a new capital called TITANPOLIS, near the volcano; he also introduces a new currency, the Calorie. In New York, Yeuse is introduced to the CANYST. Kapoul returns to the Network, while Lien and Louan continue their journey eastward towards the Southern Atlantic ice shelf.

10: The Rail Sailboats:
   Increasingly convinced that Jdrien is their prophesied god, a tribe of Redfurs launch on a perilous journey to bring the corpse of his mother, Jdrou, which has been preserved in ice, to Kamenepolis. More and more Ice Men gather there, creating political trouble with the Whalers for the Kid.
   Meanwhile, Lien and Louan experience harrowing adventures as they cross the Southern Atlantic ice shelf in a sailtrain. They are arrested by the Africanians, and Lady Diana uses pressure to ensure Lien's return. In New York, the CANYST recognizes the Kid's Company, helping to solve its economic problems; but then, Jdrien is kidnapped by Lady Diana's agents, and people wrongly accuse the Kid of having sold him to the Pan-Americans.
   Now in possession of Jdrien, Lady Diana sends the information via Yeuse to force Lien to return, but he refuses, and he and Louan continue their journey eastward on the Indian ice shelf. Meanwhile, Julius Kerr and his Sun Reclaimers have secretly relocated at Jarvis Station, located in the northern part of the Kid's Company.
   Lien and Louan arrive in Kamenepolis. The Kid and the Glaciologist make peace, and forge an alliance against Lady Diana. The Kid takes Lien to the Redfurs' enclave, where Jdrou's body, now called the "Ice Goddess," is worshipped by the Ice People.

11: The Sun Fanatics:

Lien helps the Kid begin the construction of a gigantic ice bridge that will link the Pacific Shelf Company to the American continent. Meanwhile, the Redfurs take Jdrou's body and leave Kamenepolis in search of Jdrien. Yeuse, who has been authorized to see the child, uncovers further proof of not only his telepathic powers, but also of his abilities to mentally override electronic devices.

Then, the Sun Reclaimers strike, just as the Kid, alerted by Fuerza, becomes aware of them; they open a new, larger breach in the dust cloud. The temperature rises rapidly, causing the ice to begin to melt. Chaos ensues as the Pacific Shelf Company's very survival is threatened. Miele and hundreds of others die as the ice collapses and their train is plunged into the Ocean.

The terrifying consequences of their actions causes the Reclaimers to argue among themselves. HELMUTH is unconcerned by the death toll, but Ma Kerr, GEORGE and ANN SUBA want to stop the experiment, especially since they know they don't have enough power to make the breach permanent; the group splits. In the Pan-American, Jdrien escapes, and befriends an old miner called PAVIE.

Eventually, Lady Diana strikes a bargain with the Kid to get him to destroy the Reclaimers, but because he admires their genius, he sends Lien Rag with secret instructions to save them. However, when Lien arrives at Jarvis Station, all the machines have been destroyed and the Reclaimers have left.

12: Cancer Network:

Yeuse finds Jdrien and Pavie and wants to take them back to Kamenepolis, but Lady Diana, who had promised to let them go, changes her mind when she finds evidence of Jdrien's powers. However, the child uses his abilities to force their way onto the Cancer Network, a westward Trans-Pacific line.

After helping rebuild the Pacific Shelf Company, Lien and Louan leave the Kid to return to the Trans-European under fake identities. Lien intends to pursue his investigation into the secret of the Redfurs' origin, now particularly concerned about Jdrien's future destiny as the God of the Ice People.

On the Cancer Network, Jdrien finally meets the hundred thousand Redfurs who have come to worship him; eventually, he orders them back to Kamanepolis. A series of confrontations with Lady Diana's destroyers ensues, but they are able to successfully continue their journey.

In the Trans-European, Lien and Louan stop in New Rome, where the Church's secret library may contain some of the answers they seek. They locate Hal Mern, who now works for Governor Sadon and, through him, discover a secret document which could embarrass the Church by showing that there was a break in the legitimacy of its Popes during the early years of the Ice Age -- around 2050 A.D., although for the first time, Lien finds clues that their current calendar may have been tampered with. Also, they find startling information about space travel and space colonies established by Mankind before the Ice Age.

13: Ghost Station:
Yeuse, Jdrien, Pavie and their mechanic, WARK, travel on the Cancer Network until the end of the line. They decide to build an extension to it, a long, harrowing task performed under grueling circumstances. They

stay in a vast, deserted Station, nicknamed GHOST STATION, that must have once been a thriving metropolis. But is it really deserted? They see strange shapes and Jdrien detects alien thoughts.

Meanwhile, Lien has returned to Kamenopolis, where the Kid's conflict with the Whalers has intensified. Brother Peter refuses to trade Lien's compromising document against information about the Redfurs, but instead offers to take him to the Cancer Network. After a perilous journey through forgotten lines, they are captured by a band of pirates called the JUNKMEN. Their queen, SUNNY, rapes Lien to have a child by him.

In Ghost Station, Yeuse, Jdrien and the others eventually discover the fate of the long-gone inhabitants: they have become the JONAH MEN, a race of humans living in a symbiotic state inside giant, intelligent, mutated whales—their existence a secret to all.

Lien and Brother Peter eventually make their way to the Cancer Network, where they encounter JELLY, a mysterious, huge protoplasmic entity which feeds by absorbing all living matter. They succeed in driving a railcar through Jelly and, finally, arrive in Ghost Station, where Lien and Jdrien reunite.

14: The Jonah Men:

In Ghost Station, Pavie dies. Wark decides to build a sail-powered sled and leaves, but the others, afraid of travelling on a non-railbound vehicle, refuse to accompany him. They pursue their grueling efforts to reconnect the Cancer Network to the Pacific Shelf Company's northbound 160th Meridian Line.

Hal Mern has arrived at the Pacific Shelf Company's Despair Station but cannot get an entry visa, while the Kid's conflict with the Whalers escalates. When

Wark arrives in the Company on his sailboat, the sacrilegious nature of his journey ignites severe civil strife. The Whalers kidnap the Kid; they want him to abdicate, but he refuses. Eventually, he succeeds in escaping and regroups with his followers to fight the Whalers.

In an effort to once more grab Lien and Jdrien, Lady Diana's forces invade Ghost Station but are forced to withdraw after it is sabotaged by our heroes. They, themselves, are doomed to remain imprisoned there, until the Jonah Men come out of hiding and offer to secretly transport them back to the Pacific Shelf Company, if Lien promises to have the Kid put a stop to the hunting of their whales.

When they arrive in Despair Station, Lien and his friends discover that they are forbidden entrance to the Pacific Shelf Company by the new regime -- and Hal Mern has mysteriously disappeared.

15: Terminus Despair:

In Despair Station, Lien and his friends start an armed resistance movement to help the Kid. The former leader of the Pacific Shelf Company uses the most violent means to fight against the Whalers, even sinking an entire Station into the ocean, to the dismay of LICHTEN, the Company's Master-Dispatcher. Lien also learns that Sunny has had a son by him, whom she has christened LIENSUN.

The Whalers gain Lady Diana's military support; she sends a fleet to their rescue; soon afterwards, Pan-American forces invade the Company, and Kamenepolis falls easily into their hands, unlike Titanpolis, which resists. Outside, Lien is arrested by the Mikado, who plots to deliver him to Lady Diana.

Elsewhere, the group of Sun Reclaimers still led by the Kerrs and the Subas have found another refuge. They discover that the whales used by the Jonah Men produce natural helium; they immediately plan to use this natural technology to build an airship.

The Siberians offer to help the Kid, whose armies are losing to the Pan-Americans. In a final gambit, the Kid booby-traps the ice shelf itself, and as Lady Diana launches her final offensive against the Kid's last bastion, the shelf collapses, sending the entire Pan-American fleet deep into the Ocean. Meanwhile, Despair Station falls into the hands of the C.C.P., a group of young, radical fanatics who condemn Lien to death; he is abandoned on the ice.

16: The Ice Melters:

Lien survives and discovers a lonely fishing plant whose inhabitants, the BERMANN-VERIANO family, have been long dead. He finds that they were descendents of space colonists who left Earth in 2018 A.D. on Spaceship TERRA to travel to OPHIUCHUS IV. Evidence seems to indicate that, at one point, they returned, but when and how? Further research shows that the whole family was murdered by a phony fish trader named TARPHYS.

Meanwhile, Yeuse and Jdrien search for Lien in Despair Station. Louan arrives and threatens to expose the Mikado, unless he withdraws his support for the Pan-Americans; her Company already weakened by her war with the Kid, Lady Diana must ask for a truce.

Lien eventually returns and learns that Tarphys was a Pan-American agent. He meets the current Tarphys family, who admit their ancestor killed the Bermann-Verianos on the Pan-American's orders, but refuse to reveal why. Lien feels it is all linked to the mystery of the years 2012-2200 (the current year is officially 2348). It is all linked to the Oblique Road, but if Redd Wolfe's story was only a cover-up, what is the truth?

Lien begins to feel that, if Jdrien is special, it may be because he, too, is special; maybe he is predestined to find the answers to all these mysteries. He decides to begin by looking into his own origins. Meanwhile, Lady Diana offers the Kid a lucrative deal if he surrenders Lien to her, telling him that the Glaciologist is dangerous for their world's very survival. The Kid refuses.

17: The Were-Pit:

The C.C.P. take over Kamenepolis. The Kid is determined to crush the city, which he feels betrayed him. Although he is occupied in defending himself against the liberal elements' accusations of war crimes, he secretly engineers a plot to warm up the waters beneath Kamenepolis, which will cause many more deaths and destruction, but the scheme is thwarted by Louan.

Meanwhile, the Tarphys have sent assassins after Lien. He uses the Jonah Men to flee secretly to the Trans-European, where he pursues his research into his family tree. He locates a mysterious book written by his great-great-grandmother, a woman named JUBE RAGUS, who appears to have been telepathic. Eventually, he locates the only other living descendent of his family, a legless man named LIENTY RAGUS, who raises reindeer in the Great North.

In the Pacific Shelf Company, the Sun Reclaimers steal the equipment they need to build their airship. The situation in Kamenepolis becomes more critical. The Kid sends in his troops, ending it all in a massacre. The Tarphys, who have kidnapped Hal Mern, give him to the Neo-Catholic Church.

Lienty eventually takes Lien into the radioactive pit where the were-beasts originate; at the bottom is a crashed spaceship. More troubling is the fact that the beasts obey the name of "Ragus," which they wear tattooed on their wrists.

18: The Sacrilegious Airship:

Lien Rag is arrested by Security after he leaves the Ragus farm. He is taken to Floa, who uses him as a pawn to bargain with Lady Diana, much to the dismay of the other members of the Pan-American Board (JEB INTERSON), the powerful protein manufacturer, THE VETERAN, MIRASOLA, etc. Floa leaks the news of his arrest to Kurts, who frees Lien and takes him to Skoll in the Western Zone.

Meanwhile, in the Pacific Shelf Company, the Kid appoints Yeuse to make Kamenepolis the cultural center of the planet. She charms a CANYST commission sent to inspect the Company, and produces a play by a controversial writer named R; the play takes place before the Ice Age and mentions the spaceship TERRA by name.

This comes as the Sun Reclaimers take their first experimental trip in their new airship, but are eventually caught inside Jelly. They have also been spotted by various people, rekindling the fears against them. Meanwhile, Lien looks into research being done in the Western Zone about the collective memory of the Redfur race. He finds confirmation of the Jdrien Prophecy, and the ever-present mention of the words: SALT and SUGAR—the latter being Ragus spelled backward.

While Lady Diana plots to pit the Kid against Lien, the Glaciologist and Louan prepare to return to the Pacif-

ic Shelf Company. An alarming fact is also brought to
light: temperatures are slowly mounting; in 25 years, the
ice melting point will be reached...

19: Liensun:

After Sunny's death, the Junkmen are destroyed by
other pirates, forcing Sunny's daughter, JAEL, to flee
with Liensun, who has the same telepathic powers as
Jdrien; Jael has become the prostitute of a roving gang.
They meet the Sun Reclaimers, who have finally succeeded in escaping Jelly. The gang plans to murder
them, but because they want to find Lien Rag, Jael and
Liensun help the Reclaimers to kill the gang instead.

Lien has returned to the Pacific Shelf Company and
has been reunited with Jdrien and Yeuse. He meets R,
whose play is a big success. R tells him that he is sure
the spaceship TERRA returned to Earth -- bringing other
ships with it, which may still be hidden somewhere. Lien
is now convinced his family came back on the TERRA,
and that he has been programmed to save the Ice World
by reopening the gate of space.

The Kid tells Lien that he has located Hal Mern,
who is imprisoned in a small Neo-Catholic controlled
company called HOLY CROSS. Lien prepares to set out
to rescue Mern, and has a fiberglass sailtrain built. However, he suspects a trap; further investigation shows that
the Holy Cross Company is financially supported by the
Kid—who told him about Mern. The Kid has told the
Church that if it supports him in his expansion plans, he
will deliver Lien to them.

In reality, the Kid plans to double-cross them by
preventing Lien from going, by not supplying him with
the fiberglass he needs. Unfortunately, Lien discovers

Kid's plan, and foils it by leaving for the Holy Cross Company with Louan.

20: The Dumpsters of Eternity:

With the help of the Redfurs, Lien and Louan succeed in freeing Hal Mern. His newest theory about the Ice People is that they existed in Tibet before the Ice Age. He thinks they are descendents of a group of heretics pursued by the Catholic Church in 451 A.D.—in essence, the very descendents of Christ himself. Lien is skeptical, but can see how this would gravely threaten the Church.

Later, they are captured by the Tarphys, and brought to the Dumpsters of Eternity, a small Company ruled by fanatics and dedicated to the execution of criminals. Meanwhile, the Reclaimers have adopted Liensun, and raise him as one of their own. The Kid refuses to help them, so they travel further north on the shelf to build a new base.

The Kid wants Jdrien to inherit his Company when he dies. The child puts pressure on him to help Lien, but the Kid finds himself powerless. At the Dumpster of Eternity, judgment is passed; Lien, Louan and Mern are summarily executed by being placed in a vat of water and exposed to the freezing cold.

21: The Graveyard Trains:

Ten years have passed since the previous volume. Yeuse is still in charge of Kamenepolis and has married R. The Kid, now also called President Kid, has made the Pacific Shelf Company one of the world's great powers. The Kid meets Lady Diana, whose North-South tunnel is a failure, and is looking for an alliance against the Siberians.

Liensun now leads the Reclaimers, who have built a small fleet of airships, and call themselves a DIRIGIBLE COMPANY. They wage a war of nerves with the Kid's Company. The Kid has two of their airships shot down, inflaming the situation.

Jdrien is a young man, and has never completely forgiven the Kid for betraying his father. Yeuse receives some information which makes her believe Lien may not be dead after all. Separately, she and Jdrien set out on quests to find the truth. Eventually, they meet at the Dumpster's graveyard trains, where they become lovers. They find Louan and Mern's bodies, but Lien's is missing; further clues indicate he might still be alive.

22: The Sons of Lien Rag:

Liensun has come to HOT STATION in the Pacific Shelf Company to agitate the Reclaimers Underground into committing terrorist acts, sometimes directed against the Redfurs. Liensun hates Jdrien who has come to symbolize the Ice, while he is fighting for the Sun. He uses his half-sister Jael to avoid arrest, but is eventually captured.

Meanwhile, flying whales are spotted near Titanpolis. The Kid asks Yeuse to be his ambassador in the Trans-European; she accepts, because the clues about Lien Rag's whereabouts seem to point there. She meets ZELOY, a journalist who tells her that the fanatics who ruled the Dumpster had, in fact, only pretended to kill important people. In reality, they hid them and took them to safety.

The Kid discovers that Liensun has been behind the acts of sabotage, and that he is Lien Rag's other son. Jdrien and the Redfurs attempt to force the Kid to give them Liensun, but before he can decide, the young fanatic Reclaimer escapes and uses Yeuse to secretly leave the Company.

23: Voyager Yeuse:

The Pan-American Board is no longer at Lady Diana's beck and call; they suspect that Lien Rag took the Oblique Road. Meanwhile, Yeuse has arrived in the Trans-European, which is torn by hunger riots and a rebellion in the Southern Districts. She meets Floa, who is still in control, and follows the same trail as Lien, until she learns that his ancestors came from space, and obtains a copy of his great-great-grandmother's book.

Zeloy finds Lienty Ragus's farm, but Ragus himself is gone. He also tracks down an old man from the Dumpster of Eternity who tells him that Lien's body was taken by Kurts. Next, he prepares to explore the Were-Pit with Lienty Ragus' son. Meanwhile, Yeuse meets Brother Peter, who has become a Cardinal, and PETER HOUSK, Lady Diana's agent. She learns from the Siberian ambassador, SERNINE, that Colonel Sofi is now a powerful general. She then visits the Western Zone, and sees Skoll, who is no longer in charge; the Zone is now ruled by purebred Redfur fanatics.

In the Pacific Company, the Kid exiles R, whose works are too close to the Reclaimers' ideology. With Pan-American help, Floa crushes the Trans-European revolt; when she learns that Lady Diana wants R killed, she exiles him to the Africania. Meanwhile, to free other Reclaimers, Liensun and Ann Suba use their airships to attack a Siberian penitentiary train. They rescue LI-GATH, an old friend of Yeuse's. But because they are in danger of being attacked on both sides by both the Kid and the Siberians, they use antibiotics to build a refuge within Jelly itself.

24: The Glass Urn:

Jdrien gathers a thousand Redfurs, including his new mate, VSIN, and heads north to confront Liensun; they stop when they reach Jelly. Inside the hungry protoplasmic entity, life is difficult for the Reclaimers, who must be ever vigilant to not be swallowed by the creature. Liensun and Ligath set out on a perilous, secret mission to the Siberian to steal a nuclear reactor. They succeed, but although Liensun escapes, Ligath is arrested. Later, Liensun's airship crashes in Tibet.

In the Pacific Shelf Company, a flying whale is shot and, inside, a small Jonah girl named REWA is found; the Kid soon befriends the child. Meanwhile, Sernine has told Yeuse of the existence of a SECRET HIGH COUNCIL which is more powerful than the Companies, and is made up of people who know the secrets of this world, including the true nature of the Oblique Road. Sernine tells Yeuse that, in his Company, it is secretly believed that the ice age is twenty-four centuries old, not three.

Yeuse and Zeloy, who has been severely burned by radioactivity in the were-pit, are reunited, and he tells her what he has found, including his conviction that the word "Ragus" (or "Sugar" spelled backwards) holds the key to the mysteries. Lienty's son has disappeared. Later, still wanting to find out what really happened to Lien Rag's body, Yeuse embarks on a quest for Kurts' secret base. She receives a secret message indicating that Kurts stole Lien's body to prevent Lady Diana from genetically dissecting it. The quest takes her to the Africania Company, where she is given a glass urn which supposedly contains Lien Rag's ashes -- but are they really Lien's?

25: Sun Company:

After a harrowing trek through Tibet, Liensun reaches a small Company called the SUN COMPANY, which is ruled by Helmuth, one of Kerr's old colleagues. Helmuth wants to ransom Liensun to Ma Kerr against the nuclear reactor they stole, which he will use to make another breach in the dust cloud.

Meanwhile, Lady Diana offers to have Lien's ashes analyzed, but Yeuse refuses. Later, they are stolen, and the analysis turns out negative. Yeuse pursues her diplomatic mission to the Siberian, which is now preparing to attack the Reclaimers and invade the Northern Pacific ice shelf, much to everyone else's dismay. She meets Sofi, and convinces Ligath to use her scientific skills for peaceful purposes. Sernine tells her that Lien and Kurts are alive and that they took the Oblique Road.

In the Trans-European, Zeloy is assassinated after being interrogated by Vicra. The Major now works for the Dispatchers, who are increasingly revealed to be the powerful, occult masters of the world. In the Pacific Shelf Company, Rewa continues to mentally summon the flying whales, which may expose the Jonah Men's secret, up to now shared only by Yeuse and the Kid. Lady Diana has a secret meeting with the Kid, in which she offers him membership in the High Council—and the answers to all the mysteries.

Jdrien establishes mental contact with Jelly and is able to penetrate the protoplasmic organism; after a difficult journey, he emerges in the Sun Reclaimers' camp.

26: The Siberians:

The Siberians attack the Sun Reclaimers' former camp, driving the survivors to all flee to their base inside

Jelly. Jdrien is with them, still desirous of meeting Liensun. The Siberians pursue their advance until they confront Jelly, who forces them to retreat. However, Sofi has come to realize that, if they find a way to defeat the giant amoeba, the Northern Shelf might be theirs, including all the ivory bones left behind by Jelly.

Yeuse, who is following the Siberian campaign, objects that this territory rightfully belongs to the Kid's Company. Meanwhile, with more flying whales being sighted, the Kid is forced to yield to Lichten's pressure and lets Rewa return to the Jonah Men. But for revenge, he exiles Lichten to the 160th Meridian line. In the Trans-European, the political agitation caused by Zeloy's death refuses to die down. Vicra is arrested.

Meanwhile, in Tibet, Liensun agitates the Tibetan population who live on huge, mountain-flank scaffolds, collecting lichen, against Helmuth. The old Reclaimer then threatens to open a breach in the dust cloud and unveil the "fire demon" (the sun). Liensun is almost killed by a superstitious mob, but is rescued by an airship from Ma Kerr's group. In the final battle, Helmuth and his lab are destroyed. The Sun Company is now free for the taking.

27: *The Mysterious Hobo:*

Somewhere in the Indian Ice Shelf, we meet GUS, a mysterious, legless, amnesiac hobo who is looking for the mythical CONCRETE STATION, a sort of Eldorado of the Ice World. Soon, he is being hunted by the Tarphys. Eventually, he rediscovers that his true name is Lienty Ragus.

Meanwhile, Lady Diana meets her uncle, PALAGA, who is the secret Grand-Master of the Dispatchers, one of the most powerful men in the world. He wants her to help Vicra and Lichten, who are in trouble in their own Companies. He also wants her to find out what really happened to Kurts and Lien Rag. Lastly, he wants her to have Yeuse killed, because she is beginning to know too much. His exile lifted, R returns to the Pacific Shelf Company.

In the Trans-European, Yeuse discovers that it was the Dispatchers and not Kurts who gave her the glass urn, hoping to convince her of Lien's death. Looking for what might have activated his "programming," she and Floa follow the same itinerary as that followed by Lien (in the first book on the very first day he met them, Skoll, and heard of the Oblique Road); they barely escape an assassination attempt by Pan-American hit men.

Yeuse and Floa use this to further incriminate Vicra and Lady Diana in the world's opinion. Later, Sernine tells Yeuse that they know about Lien Rag and Kurts because their agents found Kurts' fabulous locomotive, alone and deserted, at Gravel Station, a lonely station located in the middle of the Indian Ocean ice shelf.

28: The Memory Trains:

Gus, while still avoiding the Tarphys, pursues his research in the huge Library Trains of Karachi Station, which contain almost everything ever published; eventually, he finds his ancestor's book, and further clues to the location of Concrete Station.

The Siberians have found a bacterial weapon to use against Jelly. The Sun Reclaimers are forced to leave their base and follow Jdrien on the Ice Shelf, where Vsin has been waiting for him. They plan to join Liensun in the Sun Company.

In the Trans-European, Floa blackmails Lady Diana into giving her more economic assistance. A rumor that

Cardinal Peter will become the next Pope surfaces. Yeuse wonders about the calendar of the ice age: three centuries or twenty-three?

Then, she leaves the Trans-European to find Gravel Station, but it appears to be off-limits to all traffic because of the danger of radiation leaks; unconvinced, she returns to the Pacific Shelf for a brief visit with the Kid and R, then leaves once more with ENGOL, a trader, and several other men. When they arrive at Gravel Station, they find it deserted of human beings, but filled with numerous, fierce were-beasts. Soon, they are besieged by the animals.

29: The Fabulous Locomotive:

The Kid and Lady Diana have another secret meeting where they discuss Yeuse's current mission, as well as Lienty Ragus. The latter finally finds enough information about Concrete Station that takes him, too, after many adventures, to Gravel Station.

There, he meets Yeuse, who has just finished a terrifying battle with hordes of hungry were-beasts. She has also discovered Kurts' fabulous locomotive, buried under a huge sand pyramid.

In Tibet, Lien's efforts to take over the Sun Company are thwarted by the LAMAS. In the Trans-European, Vicra is condemned to twenty years in a penitentiary train, and the Siberian's Hypothesis gains exposure.

30: In The Belly of a Legend:

After defeating the were-beasts, Gus and Yeuse succeed in breaking into Kurts' fabulous locomotive. They are now sure that Lien Rag and Kurts found the Oblique Road in Concrete Station. By clever guesswork,

Yeuse unlocks the computers which control the locomotive. Then, using clues gathered by Gus, they begin their journey towards the mysterious Concrete Station.

In Tibet, the GRAND LAMA expresses the desire to meet Jdrien, so Ma Kerr's group at last decide to go to the Sun Company with the Ice Child. There, Liensun and Jdrien meet for the first time, and grudgingly learn to respect each other. The Sun Company cannot house all the Reclaimers, and they are forced to live on the huge scaffolds which flank the mountains, and pay rent by collecting lichen. Some of the Reclaimers, led by George Suba, cannot accept this and leave; Ann Suba then becomes Liensun's lover.

In the Pacific Shelf Company, the Kid learns that Cardinal Peter has become Pope under the name of Pius XIII. The new Pope's first actions are to excommunicate the Reclaimers, to confirm that the Redfurs have no soul; and to condemn the Siberian Hypothesis.

31: The Scaffolds of Fear:

When he learns of Jdrien's intention to leave and return to the Pacific Shelf Company, the Grand Lama decides to exile Liensun, who is forced to leave with Jdrien. If Liensun comes back, the lamas will order all the other Reclaimers away; Liensun has no alternative. The Grand Lama also shows evidence to Jdrien that validates the Siberian Hypothesis. He also prophecies the final return of Jdrien, someday in the future, when the Ice World will be covered in water.

Meanwhile, the Kid learns that the Church is campaigning for the sterilization of the Redfurs. The Whalers ask for authorization to hunt the flying whales, but this creates more political problems. In the north, the Siberians push Jelly ever southward. In Tibet, Liensun and Ann reluctantly accept to follow Jdrien. Jdrien's powers save Liensun and Ann from an assassination attempt by her husband, who dies instead.

Later, the new High Council meets with Lady Diana, the Kid, General Sofi, representatives of the Church, the Africania and the Australasian Companies—a Tarphys! It is revealed that the Dispatchers have the power to stop the upward climb of temperatures (by spreading more cosmic dust?) and since all the Companies' power would wane in the drowned world that would ineluctably follow the melting of the ice, they hold a supreme weapon over them.

After a perilous journey, Gus and Yeuse find Concrete Station in an isolated spot. It is like a Citadel, guarded by Redfurs and were-beasts. In fact, they discover that it "creates" new Redfurs, but they don't know how or why. Eventually, Yeuse and Gus succeed in getting the gates to open by using the password, "Ophiuchus IV."

32: *The Hungry Mountains:*

The Siberians continue to push Jelly south with their bacterial weapon, until the giant protoplasmic being invades the Kid's Company; even the Jonah Men ask the Kid to intervene to stop the amoeba. Jdrien, who has returned, offers to help. He also discovers that Vsin is pregnant and later, she has a daughter, VSIENA. Jdrien then teams up with the Jonah Men and tries to mentally force Jelly back, but she is too afraid of the Siberians. However, he manages to bring back samples of Jelly's "blood" for experimentation.

Liensun and Ann Suba continue their work for the Reclaimers from the Company of CHINA VOKSAL. They decide to free CHESTER, a famed physicist who is prisoner in a Pan-American penitentiary train, and who could solve the problem of dissipating the dust cloud. Ann Suba returns to the Scaffolds to take over the leadership of the Reclaimers when Ma Kerr dies.

Elsewhere on the Shelf, we meet FARNELLE, a woman who lives alone on the ice in an ancient cargo ship wreck. She takes in two mysterious, intelligent Redfurs, JDRIELE and JDRUCK, who appear to have been in an accident; she eventually discovers that they have gold fillings, too much knowledge for Ice Men and even access to bank accounts!

Meanwhile, Gus and Yeuse explore the inside of Concrete Station, which is deserted and entirely automated. It was built by the "Space Interventional Center" of Ophiuchus IV, presumably in an effort to help mankind adapt to and survive the rigors of the Ice World. It seems to be a nursery for Redfurs and were-beasts. Mysterious shuttle trains lead below, towards the unexplored depths of the Station. Yeuse is afraid to take one to its terminus, but Gus is not, because he believes this is where Lien and Kurts went. After his departure, Yeuse leaves and, after abandoning Kurts' locomotive, returns to the Companies.

33: The Prodigious Agony:

Liensun prepares Chester's escape by building a new airship and gathering a paratrooper commando. The Kid's scientists have found a way to immunize Jelly against the Siberians' bacterial weapon, but it means spreading the vaccine all over Jelly, for which they need Liensun because of his airship technology. Liensun agrees to do it in exchange for help in his own scheme. But Jdrien believes he can modify Jelly's own, natural, immune system, by again penetrating the amoeba.

Yeuse is kidnapped by the Tarphys and brought to Lady Diana, who treats her with great kindness. The powerful, old woman is dying, and wants Yeuse to inherit all her shares -- thus becoming the new Pan-American leader. She finds that, in her old age, Lady Diana has changed her mind, and is now praying for a return of the Sun. But her scheme has been discovered by the Dispatchers, and they are forced to flee through South America to avoid assassination.

Meanwhile, Kurts' rogue locomotive, acting under its own programming, creates chaos in the Indian Shelf. The two mysterious Redfurs take Farnelle to Gravel Station and it is revealed that the secret of the Redfurs' origin is indeed contained in the words Salt And Sugar— S.A.S. (which is a technical word for a spatial airlock).

34: They Called Me Lien Rag:

Liensun is paid to build his airship, and spread the vaccine over Jelly; Jelly is saved and is ready to counterattack the Siberians. Jdrien too has succeeded, but when he emerges from Jelly's top, he lacks the strength to cross to safety. He is rescued by Liensun, who has arrived in his airship.

In Gravel Station, Farnelle and the two mysterious Redfurs eventually meet with Kurts' fabulous locomotive; but its computer systems have now been reimprinted with Yeuse's codes, and it refuses to obey their orders. It is revealed that Jdruk is in reality Kurts, and Jdriele, Lien Rag, who have come back from the Oblique Road, mutated into Redfurs.

Lady Diana and Yeuse leave South America and escape numerous assassination attempts to arrive at New York Station. They benefit from the help of Jeb Interson and Mirasola. Also, the Kid, who has been following

239

their journey, brings economic pressure to bear to support Yeuse against the Dispatchers. Before she dies, Lady Diana has time, in front of all the officials of the CANYST, to designate Yeuse as her only heir.

SF & FANTASY

Guy d'Armen. *Doc Ardan: The City of Gold and Lepers*
G.-J. Arnaud. *The Ice Company*
Aloysius Bertrand. *Gaspard de la Nuit*
Stephen R. Bissette: (non-fiction) *Blur* (5 vols.)
Félix Bodin. *The Novel of the Future*
Didier de Chousy. *Ignis (The Central Fire)*
C. I. Defontenay. *Star (Psi Cassiopeia)*
Charles Derennes: *The People of the Pole*
Harry Dickson.*The Heir of Dracula*
 Sâr Dubnotal. *Vs. Jack the Ripper*
Alexandre Dumas. *The Return of Lord Ruthven*
J.-C. Dunyach. *The Night Orchid (Conan Doyle in Toulouse).*
The Thieves of Silence
Paul Féval: *Anne of the Isles. Knightshade. Revenants. Vampire City. The Vampire Countess. The Wandering Jew's Daughter*
Paul Féval, *fils. Felifax, the Tiger-Man*
Arnould Galopin. *Doctor Omega*
V. Hugo, Foucher & Meurice. *The Hunchback of Notre-Dame*
O. Joncquel & Theo Varlet. *The Martian Epic*
Jean de La Hire. *Enter the Nyctalope. The Nyctalope on Mars. The Nyctalope vs. Lucifer*
G. Le Faure & H. de Graffigny. *The Extraordinary Adventures of a Russian Scientist Across the Solar System* (2 vols.)
Gustave Le Rouge. *The Vampires of Mars*
Jules Lermina. *Panic in Paris. To-Ho and the Gold Destroyers*
Jean-Marc & Randy Lofficier. *Edgar Allan Poe on Mars. The Katrina Protocol. Pacifica. Robonocchio.* (anthologists) *Tales of the Shadowmen* (6 vols.). (non-fiction) *Shadowmen* (2 vols.)
Xavier Mauméjean. *The League of Heroes*
Marie Nizet. *Captain Vampire*
C. Nodier, Beraud & Toussaint-Merle. *Frankenstein*
Henri de Parville. *An Inhabitant of the Planet Mars*
J. W. Polidori, C. Nodier, E. Scribe. *Lord Ruthven the Vampire*

P.-A. Ponson du Terrail. *The Vampire and the Devil's Son*
Maurice Renard. *Doctor Lerne*
Albert Robida. *The Clock of the Centuries. The Adventures of Saturnin Farandoul*
Brian Stableford. *The Empire of the Necromancers*: *The Shadow of Frankenstein; Frankenstein and the Vampire Countess. The New Faust at the Tragicomique. Sherlock Holmes: The Vampires of Eternity. The Stones of Camelot. The Wayward Muse.* (anthologist) *The Germans on Venus. News from the Moon*
Kurt Steiner. *Ortog*
Villiers de l'Isle-Adam. *The Scaffold. The Vampire Soul*
Philippe Ward. *Artahe (The Legacy of Jules de Grandin)*

MYSTERIES & THRILLERS

M. Allain & P. Souvestre. *The Daughter of Fantômas*
Anicet-Bourgeois, Lucien Dabril. *Rocambole*
A. Bisson & G. Livet. *Nick Carter vs. Fantômas*
V. Darlay & H. de Gorsse. *Lupin vs. Holmes: The Stage Play*
Paul Féval: *The Blackcoats: The Companions of the Treasure; Heart of Steel; The Invisible Weapon; The Parisian Jungle; 'Salem Street. Captain Phantom. Gentlemen of the Night. John Devil.*
Emile Gaboriau. *Monsieur Lecoq*
Steve Leadley. *Sherlock Holmes: The Circle of Blood*
Maurice Leblanc. *Lupin vs. Holmes: The Hollow Needle. The Blonde Phantom*
Gaston Leroux. *Chéri-Bibi. The Phantom of the Opera. Rouletabille & the Mystery of the Yellow Room*
G. Marot & L. Pericaud. *Nick Carter vs. Jack the Ripper*
William Patrick Maynard. *The Terror of Fu Manchu*
Frank J. Morlock. *Sherlock Holmes: The Grand Horizontals*
P. de Wattyne & Y. Walter. *Sherlock Holmes vs. Fantômas*
David White. *Fantômas in America*

www.ingramcontent.com/pod-product-compliance
Lightning Source LLC
Chambersburg PA
CBHW060353030726
47497CB00003B/696